# The Best of CaféLit 7

# The Best of CaféLit 7

## an anthology

*Edited by Gill James*

**Chapeltown Books**

British Library Cataloguing in Publication Data

A Record of this Publication is available from the British
Library

ISBN 978-1-910542-40-8

This edition published 2018 by Chapeltown Books
Manchester, England

# Contents

# Readers' Choice

We asked readers to vote for their give favourite stories published on the CaféLit web site in 2017. We awarded five points for number one choices, four for number two and so on.

The following stories received votes and are listed in the order of which ones received the most votes.

Authors were not allowed to vote for their own stories but we didn't mind if their friends did.

It's quite a tall order, anyway, to ask people to read all the stories published in one year but a few did and these are the results.

Next year, for The Best of CaféLit 8, we'll ask those who appear in this volume to vote.

# White Socks

## Gail Aldwin

### *Egg nog*

I tie the cord of my dressing gown. I've grown so much the sleeves come right up to my elbows. Mummy says it doesn't matter that it's a bit small, it's not as if I'm going to wear it outside for the neighbours to see. Walking down a couple of stairs, I loop the fraying edge of the carpet around my toes. The fourth step's warm from the pipes underneath and I stand, listening for the gurgle from the boiler. There's a smell of burnt toast coming from the kitchen. Mummy says bugger and the sash window judders – I bet she's scraping the bread and tipping the black crumbs outside. This happens quite often in our house.

There's no school this week so me and Paul are taking it easy. He's reading a comic in bed but Mummy has to get up because there's Daddy to look after. It's not long until he leaves for work. The coins in his jacket clink as he swings it off the back of his chair and he finds his coat hanging on the stand. He sees me on the stairs but he doesn't say anything – he nods at me and calls goodbye to Mummy. Now I know it's safe to go all the way down.

The door to the lounge is closed. This is unusual, we don't normally shut doors in our house. Grandma says we ought to be ashamed of ourselves for all the heat we waste, but when she's not around, Mummy says it doesn't matter and that they've more important things to worry about. I push the door and peak inside. The Christmas tree's in the corner and a few bits of foil twinkle. Switching on the light, I see the floor's covered with carrier bags, and tissue paper, ribbon and felt. There's one green bag with gold writing from Marks and Spencer. Lined up by the wall are a couple of baskets. Paul is written in red letters on one, the other says Sus, that must be for me, it's meant to say Susan. There's some folded clothes, it looks like a pink jumper and there are two pairs of socks turned into balls. White socks, long ones, they must be for me. I've been praying for white socks; I'm sick of getting teased for wearing my brother's old grey ones. My heart thumps in my chest. I know I shouldn't be here, shouldn't be looking. There's been some kind of mistake. It isn't Christmas for another two days. I swallow down the lump in my throat and shut the door.

On the kitchen table, the toast rack's empty, but the cereal box is open. Yesterday Paul found the plastic toy but he didn't eat any crispies, he had porridge. I told Mummy it wasn't fair, you've got to eat the crispies to get the prize, but she said not to fuss and that life's not fair. Mummy's sitting on a stool over by the oven and the door's wide open, making the room warm. The washing's hanging from the ceiling on something called a Sheila's maid. I'm glad it's not called a Susan's maid. Mist covers the windows and I draw a flower to decorate the space, drips running down my finger.

'Time for breakfast.' Mummy closes the book. 'Go and get Paul. Tell him to come down right away.'

In our room, my bed is against the short wall, and Paul's is against the long wall. At night, light peeps through the slit in the curtains and I can see him. Sometimes we whisper to each other, if he's awake and I'm awake. If there's a row going on downstairs and you can't sleep through that. Mummy says it's the drink that makes Daddy shout and when that happens I curl up like a snail, pull the covers around my neck and stare into space. I like to know where my knees and my legs are, it doesn't do to spread. You don't keep warm when you spread.

Paul throws back the cover and jumps into his slippers now that there's food to be had. He rushes downstairs still reading his comic. I don't know how he does that without bumping into something. The door to the lounge is still closed, but Paul doesn't notice there's anything strange. I'm sorry that I looked in. Mummy says when you've done something wrong it's best to own up but I'm not so sure. I usually keep quiet when something's gone wrong and I'm under suspicion. This makes Daddy angry and he shakes his fist. When I cry Mummy hugs me and then she sends me off to bed with a prod. It's strange going to bed in the middle of the day.

In my bowl is a mountain of crispies and a moat of milk. I pour sugar from the shaker and make a crust on top. Grandma hisses whenever she sees how much sugar I take but Mummy says I've got a sweet tooth, just like her. Paul's still reading the comic, the pages shake when he laughs and his shoulders go up and down. Swinging my legs, I tap the tiles on the floor and try not to hit the cracks. The flower I drew on the window has disappeared into a stripey mess.

I finish my breakfast and I look around for Mummy but she's not in the kitchen. I slosh my empty dish around in the washing up water and lean across the sink to reach for the mop with the shaggy head. Once I've finished, I turn the bowl upside down on the draining board. I rub the spoon and check it's clean by staring into the shiny bit. In the reflection, I see my cheeks are puffed like a gerbil's, and my fringe covers my eyes.

'You're looking at yourself again.' says Paul.

'No.' I put the spoon in the cutlery drawer.

Mummy rushes into the room, the flares on her trousers flapping. I wish I had a trouser suit like that. It's purple with a tunic that goes right up to her neck. Daddy ordered it from the catalogue especially for Christmas, but he's let her wear it a few times already.

'Have either of you been in the lounge this morning?' Mummy holds her forehead in her hand.

'Not yet,' says Paul. 'But I want to watch the telly later.'

I squeeze the dishcloth and the droplets splatter.

'What about you Susan?'

I get busy cleaning up.

'Have you been into the front room?'

'No.' I look at the taps when I answer.

'That's good,' she says. 'Just give me a few minutes, then you can watch telly all day if you want to. Special treat for Christmas.'

'Yippee,' says Paul.

'Oh.' I wonder what has happened to all the special things on the floor.

'You better get dressed,' says Mummy.

The lounge door's open when we come back downstairs and everything's tidy. The curtains are open and the lights on the tree flash. But there's no clothes, no white socks anywhere. They've gone, they've vanished. I hope I haven't spoilt our Christmas and that they'll be no presents for anyone. Perhaps it's my fault. I walk up the stairs, tears dripping from my eyes. Beside my pillow I find Blue Ted, we sit on the floor and I squeeze him so tight that I can't breathe.

Daddy's in a good mood when he gets home. He says he's only got one more day to work until he has a well-earned rest. Hugging Mummy, he tucks his neck onto her shoulder and he dances with her, shuffling from side to side. She giggles, his whiskers are tickling, she says. They cuddle for a bit, then Daddy sees me staring, and he lets go of Mummy. They stand holding hands, like they're going to play ring-a-ring-a-roses.

'I've got more good news for you Alan,' Mummy says. 'A card arrived from my mother today.' She nods towards the one with three camels on it. Daddy walks to the mantlepiece. He doesn't even look at the picture, he's more interested in the piece of paper that falls out. 'D'you think that's enough to pay for everything?' Daddy nods and puts the paper in his wallet. 'It's a relief, isn't it? Now we can enjoy Christmas without worrying.' Daddy says yes and asks if the kettle's boiled.

On Christmas morning, we're not allowed out of our room until it's seven o'clock. Paul's in charge of the time, and I have to wait until he says it's okay to look for our presents. I huddle in my bed while Paul chatters about the Scalextric he hopes he'll get. Maybe I imagined seeing the room all covered with papers and the presents. Perhaps it was a dream. My heart pumps as the hand on the clock moves closer and when Paul shouts we race along the passage.

'Wow,' he says. 'There's a great big box under the tree. I bet that's for me.'

Mummy and Daddy follow us into the lounge. We can open the gifts from Father Christmas, but not the ones under the tree. Not yet, anyway. Mummy passes me a pink pillowcase and Paul has the blue one. There's lots of lumpy things inside, and I pull out the basket first. The red letters say Susan, that's better, I think.

'What's this for?' Paul takes his out.

'It's a waste paper basket,' says Mummy. 'Not many children have their own, personalized waste paper basket. You can put your rubbish in there. Drawings that you don't want anymore, sweet wrappers, things like that.'

'That'll be useful,' says Paul.

Inside my basket there's another present, tied with ribbon. I undo the bow and the paper falls open. I see the socks. The same ones from the other day. Long and white.

'Do you like them?' asks Mummy.

'Yes.' I cross my arms and hold them next to my heart. 'They're just what I wanted.'

'Funny how Father Christmas always knows what you want,' says Mummy. Daddy's laughing and coughing at the same time. She gives him a little tap on the wrist and he becomes quiet. I open another present, and there's my pink jumper. I'm pleased and confused. Nothing's a surprise.

'What's up?' says Mummy. 'You look sad.'

'I'm not sad.'

'She's always been ungrateful, that little cow,' says Daddy.

I feel the tears coming and Mummy strokes my cheek.

'Whatever's the matter?' she asks.

'Nothing.' I gulp. 'But are you sure all these things come from Father Christmas?'

## About the author

Gail Aldwin is a prize-winning writer of short fiction and poetry. Cast Iron Productions (Brighton) staged *Killer Ladybugs*, a short play Gail co-wrote in 2017. As Chair of the Dorset Writers' Network, Gail works with the steering group to support writers by connecting creative communities across the county. She enjoys teaching creative writing and is a visiting tutor at Arts University Bournemouth. Her collection of short fiction *Paisley Shirt* was longlisted in the best short story category of the Saboteur Awards 2018.

# Safe

## Laura Gray

### *Tequila Sunrise*

Head down in the whistling wind, she pedalled along the low causeway that connected a necklace of sub-tropical islands flung off the southern coast. The sun was just sliding up on the eastern side, its rays picking out the wading birds in the shallows. Doubled over, she didn't hear the warning bell or see the flashing red lights until the road started to rise up in front of her. *Shit. Drawbridge. Gonna be late.*

As she slowed, another bicycle pulled up beside her. The bridge rose up to 90 degrees, blocking the view ahead, so she glanced over at the rider. His head glistened mahogany in the early sun, his long grey hair was pulled back in a ponytail. She was already ticking the boxes in her head: ragged cut-offs, disintegrating sandals, faded Hawaiian shirt flapping over countable ribs, bundles of possessions attached to each side of his bike, small sea-sprayed dog in the front basket. *Homeless person*, she thought, and looked away.

She couldn't tell if he returned her gaze, but what would he see if he did? Fiftyish square-built woman, ropy muscles, trailing tattoos down her legs. Helmet covering short curly hair, never to be a flowing ponytail. And what wouldn't he see? The endless struggle to control her movements, to control her fear, to watch for danger; anxiety flooding her body with every unexpected sound or turn of events. He wouldn't be able to tell that this drawbridge delay was torture, and the presence of another person an almost unbearable threat.

She'd got the job looking after the tourist boats, turning up early every day (*except today, dammit*). It was perfect; no people to talk to, no one came near her once she had her job sheet for the day. As long as she painted, scraped and cleaned, she was safe and in control. She'd kept the appearance of a normal life, hiding the battles she'd fought since leaving the hospital.

'Can't see anything coming through,' he said. Hyper-alert, she jumped. *Deep breath, fight the panic.*

'What do you mean?'

He jerked his head towards the bridge. 'It's been up awhile – can't see anything big enough. What do they want to keep us here for?'

She saw he was breathing heavily, sweat starting to roll. The dog looked up into his face. Something was wrong. Her clammy hands slipped on the handlebars. *I really do not need to get stuck next to a headcase*, she thought. Now she was hemmed in, with a vertical road in front, cars behind, and the waters on either side below.

She looked down over the low side railings to the flat calm water, seeing the fishing boats and canoes crawling back and forth like kids' toys. But in the distance: a large yacht, sail furled and thin mast scratching the belly of the sky.

She pointed. 'That won't get through.' Her voice wobbled as she tried to fight the terror for both of them. 'I guess they're holding the bridge for her.'

He shook his head, and she could smell the fear. His or hers?

'No way – they've got us here now. Gotta find another beach.' He wheeled his bike so suddenly that he nearly lost the dog, leaving her trapped, alone, shaking. As he went, she caught a glimpse of the miniature plate on the back of his bike: a Purple Heart, and the motto 'Combat Wounded'.

She opened her mouth to call out to him, she wasn't sure what. 'I'm sorry!' or even: 'I'm going with you!'. Too late now, he was gone, weaving between the stationary cars.

He almost made it to the end of the causeway where it joined the sand, then his bike glanced off the side of a massive Hummer. Man, bike and dog flew over the railings and onto the beach below. People, some with Smartphones at the ready, started to get out of the stopped cars. *Oh no, you don't*, she thought. Her strong legs pedalled furiously, and she beat them to it. Flinging her bike down, she hurdled the railing and landed beside him. A surprisingly short jump onto a stinking pile of seaweed.

She rolled on top of him to block the view from

above, then realised that there was a fair bit of noise and movement going on underneath her. She had instinctively wanted to protect the dead from prurient onlookers, but found she was holding down a struggling man and the growling dog in his arms. He didn't have a chance; she outweighed him by about 20 pounds, so she eased back. 'Winded,' he gasped, then curled over and vomited. The dog seemed to have decided that she wasn't a threat; it stopped growling and turned to lick the man's face.

Without raising his head, he extended a hand. 'Dave,' he said. Hesitant at first, she eventually completed the handshake. 'Sandy.' He released her hand, and then pointed at the dog, which had begun an investigation of the seaweed twined in his hair. 'Barney.' She nodded to acknowledge them both.

Dave slowly pulled himself up to a sitting position. He looked at her, then up at her sturdy bike, leaning where she had flung it against the railing. He gestured towards the pieces of his machine, spread around the sand. 'Don't suppose you'd give me a lift to the bike shop?' He looked away. She was pretty sure he'd sensed her fear, her reluctance to make contact. His tone sounded resigned, expecting rejection. Barney, equally sensitive it seemed, folded his tail between his legs, and slunk behind Dave.

To her surprise, there was no hesitation this time. She and her bike were strong enough for all of them, so she helped him to his feet. Man, woman and dog headed back towards the railings. Unobserved now; the yacht had gone through, the bridge had gone down, and the audience had retreated.

As they made their way slowly across the sand, she bent and picked up the dog's basket from where it had been hurled in flight. The basket was unexpectedly heavy. Puzzled, she looked down and saw the gun nestling in a side pocket. Her eyes closed, and she breathed a sigh of relief. Wherever they were headed, at least she knew she'd be safe.

**About the author**
Laura Gray has returned to writing after retirement. Her previous publications have been as Features Editor of her high school newspaper in the 1960s. She is greatly enjoying the challenge of fiction and poetry.

# Do Pigeons Ever get Bored?

## Robin Wrigley

### *Fortified wine*

'Are you alright Oliver?' Blast, it was the verger's wife Mrs Mutton wandering through the churchyard and there was no lookout to give us our coded warning – 'Baaaa'.

Gerald Godfrey or 'Horse' as he was known to his friends and I were lying in the poorly maintained, long grass, the result of the verger Mr Mutton being off sick with a bad back. We were trying to hit pigeons in the yew trees with marbles fired from my catapult.

'We were watching the pigeons and wondering if they ever get bored Mrs. Mutton.' It was all I could think off the top of my head and no warning. At that moment we were saved as the first bell began ringing for Morning Prayer.

'You boys really have some daft ideas Oliver. But there is the bell so you'd better get yourself into the vestry and get changed before the choirmaster is out here looking for you. Go on – do pigeons ever get bored, whatever next?'

'Phew that was close, Horse,' I whispered as we got up and ran to the back door of the vestry stuffing my catapult into my blazer pocket as we went.

Inside the vestry the creep, Melvin Walton was

pulling the bell rope making it look like it was some form of a dark art when in fact anybody could do it. I even did it one Evensong when I happened to be the first there to volunteer and Walton was away.

Fifteen minutes later and we were all in cassocks, surplices and ruffs and positioning ourselves in two lines behind the creep Walton who not only claimed the position of bell-ringer, but also the carrier of the stave and brass-cross leading us two by two up the aisle.

This is the part I liked best as we silently walked up between the assembled parishioners trying our best to look meek and mild while sneaking looks to the nearest pews to see if there was any new young girls present. Horse and I led behind the creep with me on the left in order to peel off left and get the nearest seat on the left-hand pew and the best view of the congregation.

Our choir-master and organist, crabby Crabbe was bashing away on the organ using the mirror placed above so he could see us filing into place and when to end his opening piece. His playing was quite amusing, pushing and pulling various stops, playing the keyboard in a very dramatic way, his head moving in time with the music. His antics, swaying and exaggerated hand movements making it look as though he was on some famous stage rather than hidden behind the choir stalls where only the choirboys opposite could see him. He loved these opening pieces, they were his pride and joy and he attacked them with gusto. It was the only time he ever appeared to be really happy.

Once the last of the grown-up singers were in position behind us trebles and the creep had secured the stave and cross, made a big deal over his genuflection as though he was Gregory Peck or something while we prepared to lower the hinged choir-stall seat into position.

It was at this point when my plan to ogle the blonde girl in the front pew went horribly wrong. The bench seat we seven choirboys sat on hinged up until we were all ready to sit down; when the time came for us to sit we lowered the seat onto three wooden brackets. I was sitting over one of the end brackets and my longest finger got trapped between the seat and the bracket.

How I managed not to scream out I will never know. Trying to explain with nudges and sign language to six idiot choirboys to get up sufficiently for me to get my finger free took forever. Close to fainting, leaving the stall from the side nearest the congregation, I quickly crossed myself and shot towards the altar and out of the other side door by old Crabbe. I could sense him glaring at me with that look of his that we all knew so well from rehearsals.

Once out in the open churchyard I was able to let out a huge yell and burst into tears. My right hand long finger was white, twice its normal width and hurting like I have never felt in my life. My yell must have alerted Mrs Mutton who came shuffling round the corner with a sickle in her hand. Scared and frightened as I was I thought she was going to attack me and I cowered away from her.

'What on earth are you yelling about Oliver, what the Dickens is wrong with you and why are you out here?' I couldn't speak, words wouldn't come out I continued crying and hung my hand up to show her my injured finger.

'Well boy, that be God's retribution for attacking his innocent birds and telling lies. That's what that be.'

**About the author**
Robin was a late-comer to writing fiction having joined a local writers' group in his early seventies. He has spent most of his adult life in foreign countries, over twenty in all, initially as a land surveyor and later in the geophysical exploration for oil. His experiences have given him a wealth of potential stories. However, transposing thoughts to the written word and the qwerty keyboard have now replaced the hazards he encountered in hostile environments.

# Murmuration

## Fiona Mills

*Home-made elderflower with sparkling water*

'Let me take you under my wing,' you said, 'together we will ride the thermals, reach heights you never imagined.' So I flew the nest, leaving behind all family and friends.

'We are swans,' he said, 'paired for life, needing no-one but each other.' I thought we were turtle doves.

We flew around the globe, just the two of us, stopping long enough to say we'd seen life, but never long enough to live. And for a time I was happy to listen only to your call. We watched as others defined their territory, built their nests and raised their young.

'How lucky we are to soar above those ordinary lives!'

But then I heard it. The beat of a thousand wings in perfect harmony; a murmuration, a moving tableau in the sky. How did the common starling, so raucous, so angular, create such beauty? I felt its ripples overwhelm me.

'Don't leave,' you said, 'I cannot live alone.'

But you are not my swan or my turtle dove. You are an albatross, loyal to the end, but content to live on the wing. You are weighing me down and I can no longer fly.

And so I leave and join the dance. I swoop, I soar,

I find myself in the crowd. I am, it turns out, a home-bird after all.

*Note: The male albatross spends many years choosing a partner, and remains loyal till one of them dies. It is not part of a flock, and only joins others to select a mate and breed.*

**About the author**
Fiona is a freelance radio journalist and mum of three who has always secretly longed to write fiction.

# Waiting for Pogo

## Penny Rogers

### *Breakfast tea – well brewed*

'This is outrageous, utter rubbish, and you are an imposter.' A small crowd gathered around the formidable figure of Mrs Portiboys and the slight, rather exotic young woman that she was addressing. Aware of the interest her outburst had caused, the older woman lowered her tone. 'Go away,' she hissed. 'You are nothing to do with my brother. If you do not go immediately I will call a policeman.'

The girl replied nervously in heavily accented English, 'Please listen to me, I can explain.'

The clock on St Martin-in-the-Fields struck eleven. Thirty years was a long time to wait for anyone, even the brother who had meant so much to her. She considered the girl carefully, and for once she changed her mind.

'All right young woman, but you have got some explaining to do. And not here.' People around them were drifting back to their normal business.

At the base of the steps to the National Gallery a newspaper vendor shouted 'Evening News! Russian ships going to Cuba. Evening News!'

Mrs Portiboys shuddered; nuclear war was looming. 'I suggest we go for a cup of tea.' They walked in silence towards the Strand.

Something about the hoarse cries of the newspaper seller resonated in her memory, Father's angry voice shouting dreadful words most of which she did not understand at the time. She recalled doors slamming, her mother's cry and the silence that followed Pogo's departure.

The two women reached the Lyons Corner House at the end of the Strand and found a table near the window. As she had done so many times before, Mrs Portiboys carefully positioned herself facing the street and the direction of Trafalgar Square. She clutched at the remnants of her fast dwindling hope that one day he would be there, just slightly delayed. The Nippy came for an order. 'Two teas' she snapped, quickly adding 'Please' as the waitress turned away.

'We gotta trust Mr Kennedy,' an American accent momentarily rose above the subdued murmur of the cafe 'The President'll hold his nerve.'

The young woman took the initiative 'My name is Elena; I am your brother Paul's daughter.'

'So I know you are a liar. He cannot have any children.' Years of practice kept her voice steady, but her thin lips all but vanished into her trembling mouth. Their tea arrived and she carefully poured out two cups. 'But seeing as we are here you'd better go on with your story. Before I call the police' she added.

'My father told me that when he left home he

promised to meet you on his birthday, at eleven o'clock on October 23 by the empty plinth in Trafalgar Square.' Mrs Portiboys thought to herself whoever she is, she has done her homework. Out loud she said 'So why are you here and not him?'

'Sadly my father died last year. He had been ill for some time.' Mrs Portiboys felt a wave of sadness, but after so long her sorrow was tempered with relief. Thirty years was a long time to wait, and here was some sort of resolution. She was starting to believe the girl. 'He lived in Argentina,' continued Elena 'he emigrated there after he left England.'

In her handbag Mrs Portiboys had a photograph of Pogo. It was the only one she had. Her late husband, the Colonel, had not approved of photographs; he was not a sentimental man. Although Pogo had left two years before she even met the Colonel, he had made his disapproval of both photographs and his missing brother-in-law very clear.

In recent years she had wondered if she would even recognise her brother. The woman claiming to be his daughter looked nothing like him. Mrs Portiboys was wary again; suspicious that some sort of trick was being played on her.

'So, if you are indeed my niece why do you look so, well…' she uncharacteristically fumbled for the right words, 'so… Spanish? Who is your mother?'

Elena sighed. 'I don't know. I lived in an

orphanage until I was two. Then your brother adopted me. I was just one of a large number of children in orphanages in Buenos Aires. Many never left, some ended up in sweat shops or prostitution and a few were adopted. The authorities were just glad to see a child go. To any sort of family; they did not ask too many questions.'

The Nippy placed the bill in front of them.

'Shall we walk for a little while?' It was more a command than a question. They negotiated their way across Trafalgar Square, through groups of people anxious for news of the drama unfolding on the other side of the Atlantic.

Mrs Portiboys remembered when Pogo was born. There had been a governess who took her for walks and talked about the baby. He was almost two weeks old before she was allowed to see him. Father told her that one day this tiny baby would be a great soldier and that she must help Mama look after him.

She had spent hours reading to him, playing games, telling stories, even writing a play for them to act in front of their governess. It was never an imposition, he was simply her life. Paul Hugo seemed a big name for such a small child and she always called him Pogo, much to the irritation of her parents. For years Mrs Portiboys had never mentioned her beloved brother to anyone. She had tried once. Not long after she married, with all the confidence of a new bride she had asked her parents if they knew where Paul was. Her father retreated behind The Times. Her mother looked directly at her and said 'Paul? I don't know anyone named Paul.'

'Why didn't he contact me?' Mrs Portiboys fixed Elena with a cold stare. The young woman responded gently 'I don't think even he could answer that. Time goes on and in the end I think he just kept you in a secret corner of his mind.'

'Yet he must've known that I would come here every year in all weathers to wait for him.' She was irritated that her brother had not kept his promise.

'He only saw your advert a few years ago.' Elena knew how lame this sounded, so she carried on quickly 'One day he bought a mirror that was delivered wrapped in an old copy of The Times. He flattened it out and read it, every word. Then he reached the Personal Column and he saw a message from you. It was the only time I saw him cry.'

'Yet he still did not get in touch.' Mrs Portiboys shook her head with disappointment.

Elena sensed the older woman's sadness. 'He did mean to, but the newspaper he saw was five years old. He wasn't sure of your surname, or where you lived. He only knew that you were keeping your promise.'

Mrs Portiboys recalled the awful arguments, the hurtful words and eventually the realisation that her parents would never understand, or forgive, their son. She had never spoken about their rift with her brother to anyone, so she had to struggle to find the words. 'Father wanted Pogo to be a soldier like him. He had ambitions for him, a glorious career in his old regiment. He was so proud when Pogo did well at school. They had a huge row when Pogo refused to go to Sandhurst.' She still could not mention the final confrontation, when Pogo dropped his bombshell and walked out of their lives.

She turned to Elena 'Your father was a fine man.'

Elena paused before carefully continuing. 'Then he became ill and could not travel. So I promised him I would come and find you. Here I am.' She looked tired and cold; the anxious crowds pressing around them clearly disturbed her. Mrs Portiboys noticed that her companion was shivering. She relented. 'I think I believe your story, but there are still many questions to be answered. Shall we go and find some lunch?'

Later she retrieved the precious photo from her handbag. 'Do you have a more recent picture of your father?' She hesitated as the treasured photo was passed across the table.

Elena took a wallet out of her bag. From it she retrieved a photograph and passed it to her aunt. The picture showed a laughing man with curly hair. It was clearly Pogo. Standing by his side was a tall man wearing sunglasses. The tall man's hand was on Pogo's shoulder. She took a deep breath. 'Who is the other man?'

'That's Maxwell.' Elena's eyes lit up. 'I still have one father. I am very lucky. He knows that I am here.' She hesitated. 'He asked that if I found you I should pass on his respects to you.'

Mrs Portiboys said nothing. She took a crisp handkerchief from her bag and discreetly blew her nose.

**About the author**
Penny writes short stories, flash fiction and poetry and tries to keep her blog updated. She has been published in anthologies including *Henshaw, The Best of CaféLit* and *This Little World*, as well as in (and on) *Paragraph Planet, Bare Fiction, Writers' Forum, A Million Ways* and *South*.

https://pennyrogers.wordpress.com

# The First

## Richard Hough

### *Espresso, extra shot*

I never knew her name though her face haunts me still. When I entered the waiting room at Winchester's railway station, she was already there, sitting alone, staring into the past. The first thing I noticed about her was those beautiful, sapphire-blue eyes. Even in my student days, when Frankie was telling us to Relax and Band Aid was wondering if 'they' knew it was Christmas, I was attracted by a woman's eyes above any other physical feature; it was what initially drew me to my wife some ten years after this brief encounter.

Closing the door to keep out the fumes of passing diesel trains, I tried to avoid any awkwardness by greeting the stranger with a cheery 'hello!'

A sad, wizened face turned towards me and I was immediately reminded of my boyhood neighbour who constantly complained about me and made my life a misery. How I hated that old hag. This traveller dourly returned my greeting.

'Goot evenink,' she murmured. It was then I saw something, deep within those eyes. Torment was present; heartache perhaps for a lost lover? No, that wasn't it. It was pain of a much different kind.

Having been raised in Birmingham, I was used to

meeting people from different ethnic backgrounds. Many were, for example, immigrants from India and Pakistan. My closest boyhood friend was of Afro-Caribbean origin but I had never encountered anyone with an accent such as this stranger possessed. I seized upon the novelty to strike up a conversation which would have such a lasting impact on the rest of my life.

After we had exchanged the usual pleasantries concerning the weather and interminable delays to the Sunday train timetables, I grew a little braver.

'Excuse me for being rude but I'm guessing you aren't local. May I ask where you're from?'

'I am Russian but I haf lived in Enkland for many years.'

Being inquisitive, I wanted to know more about her homeland.

'How olt are you?' she demanded, those sorrowful eyes looking into mine. I replied I was to remain a teenager for just a few weeks more.

She explained when she was my age she lived in abject poverty in Petrograd, the Russian capital at the time. Her father had gone off to fight Germany but the superior fire power of the German army had proved too much for her countrymen whose morale was already low. Many Russians were killed, her own father never returning from the war. Czar Nicholas II (she almost spat the name) lived in luxury whilst she and so many ordinary people went hungry. The people in the capital city of this huge country had virtually nothing to eat, even bread being in short supply. Their leader was weak; all he could do was to keep dissolving parliament, each time to little or no effect.

The winters were always cold and harsh and eventually people took to the streets in anger and frustration. As those steely eyes stared into mine, a tear formed. Her ageing, husky voice almost faltered as she explained why she had joined that awful revolution. She had seen so many terrible things in March 1917. Men did such awful things to each other, things which surely no deity could reasonably forgive. Worse followed until even soldiers eventually deserted their leader.

As a young, hungry woman who had lost her father and had younger siblings to help feed, this tormented soul had joined the forces of rebellion. The horrors she had only previously witnessed from afar, she became guilty of committing herself. Those same atrocities she had condemned before hunger had consumed her sense of morality. She forfeited her eternal soul to help replace one form of tyranny with another and it was the futility of this which distressed her most, a view she readily voiced.

Even now she was elderly she still could not forget the abhorrence of those times. They haunted her dreams but worse, they pursued her wherever she went. Her people, she said, sacrificed so much for nothing more than endless years of new horrors. She prayed daily her countrymen would once again be at liberty.

As the tears came more freely from those tired, angst-ridden eyes, this stranger whom I suddenly knew so well, implored me to enjoy my freedom and live without hatred. I knew I could help her end the nightmares.

I often relive every detail of that evening wondering if the woman, whose name I never asked, found peace when I closed her eyes for the last time. Since then I have supplied an end to many other stories but this is the one I remember most, my first.

**About the author**
Richard Hough has been writing since he had a joke published in his favourite boyhood comic, Sparky. He has self-published one novel and is currently working on a second in the spare time which eludes him almost completely. He has a wife, two sons and two cats choose to live with them for the time being.

# Bottled Christmas Spirit

## Derek Corbett

### *Single malt*

I remember that Christmas a couple of years ago as if it were yesterday. The names of those involved in making the WW1 film, where at the end soldiers from both sides meet up to sing 'Silent Night,' was still scrolling on the screen when Amy, my son Jack's fiancée at the time said.

'It's Morecombe and Wise next. It's a repeat, but still it'll be a good laugh.'

That's when my mum asked where her grandson was. I still remember the concerned look on Grandad's face as her told her.

He left just a moment ago. Didn't look to clever either. I reckon it could have been the film.'

Taking off her glasses she looked towards the lounge doorway.

'I didn't see him leave do you reckon he's alright?'

That was enough to prompt Amy to get up and move towards the door announcing.

'His 'Post Traumatic thingy' has been bothering him a bit today. I'd better check.'

Even though it was twelve months since he'd had to retire from the Army, he was still trying to come to terms with his tours in Iraq and Afghanistan. It had us watching him like a hawk which is why his mum followed Amy out the room.

Reappearing a few minutes later, Amy announced. 'We've checked every room in the bungalow and his coat's gone.'

'Maybe he's popped out for a walk round the Orchards,' suggested his gran. Moments later, knowing the problem he was still trying to come to terms with, his grandad and I, overcoats and hats on with orders to find him, were hurrying across the bitterly cold yard. Half way to the gate that leads out to Pipp's Apple and Plum Orchards, our family business Dad said.

'We don't really need torches.'

I guess that like me he was worried and felt he had to say something. Even though it was obvious our presence had triggered the automatic floodlight system, making the yard brighter than daytime. As we reached out to open the gate that led into the first field, the system timed out, leaving us in darkness.

Dad touched me on the shoulder and pointed towards the packing shed as I reached for the torch in my pocket.

'There's a light in the shed, Bill.'

We walked quickly to the door and entered. Although there was no sign of Jack, we did see the rope complete with noose hanging from a beam.

'Jack,' I called out, 'you OK son?'

It was stupid question really, what with his recent behaviour. Immediately he appeared from one of the packing bays and stood there with an expression, somewhere between sheepishness and annoyance, on his face. Without saying a word his grandad walked up to him and flung his arms around him. Immediately the lad began to cry. I looked over the boy's shoulder and his granddad and I saw that like me, he had tears rolling down his cheeks.

'What we going to do?' I mouthed.

Dad blinked and shook his head.

I knew I couldn't take him back to his mum in that state, so I suggested that we go and sit in the office for a bit. I switched on the electric fire and took out my almost full bottle of whisky from the filing cabinet. I whipped out three used mugs, and poured a generous helping into each.

'Now this is what I call Christmas spirit,' joked Dad a little later as we sat around the desk sipping our whisky. 'Single Malt, your taste must have improved Bill, after the stuff you used to drink.'

Once again Dad was talking just for something to say, for when he ran the business up to a year ago; it had been his whisky we drank. Then Dad suddenly looks at his grandson and says, 'Do we have a serious problem, Jack?'

I thought it was being a bit blunt, but then Dad always was a bit of a straight talker. 'Haven't the people at the MOD place been able to help you?'

Jack nodded without looking up.

'A bit but I still get really bad days.'

'And you reckon what you have out there, will answer your problem?'

'I guess so,' he mumbled.

'OK, well I can see why it would be a solution, but before you go any further I'd like to tell you something about your family history, if you will listen. Will you listen? I mean really listen?'

Jack nodded and looked up.

'Yes,'

'Good. Bill a touch more of that whisky, if you please.'

Having no idea what he was about to say, I just added to the three mugs.

'Nearly 100 years ago after the 14-18 punch up, your great-great-grandad, came back from three years in the trenches. Like you, he too had memories, as well as having lost some toes from foot rot. When he got home he met and married your great-great-grandmother. I remember her she was one strong minded woman. She talked him into renting and then buying a few fields, with some run down apple and plum trees in them. Time went by; they had three sons and those fields became the start of the Orchards we work today. Then World War II started and my dad and his two brothers were called up. My dad was the only one to survive. Like you, he came home trying to forget. It was your great-great-gran and grandad got him through it. He married your great-gran and they had me. Against their advice I too joined the army. In fact I enjoyed it so much I finished up with some special outfit helping the Yanks in Vietnam. Your gran will tell you how many times my nightmares have woken her.'

Then it was your dad's turn. Unfortunately he came home from the Falklands not only with bad memories but also with half a leg missing. You don't need me to tell you how well he has come to terms with that.'

'I suppose what I'm trying to say is that some things take a while to come to terms with. But the choices we make to cope with them do not have to be made on our own. That's what families are for, to help you make a choice or even to give us a shoulder to cry on.

Jack's grandad, pointed towards the packing bays.

'Out there, is one solution to your problem. Unfortunately it doesn't solve the problems of those that love you and are left behind. Do you see where I'm coming from son?'

Jack remained looking into his mug a moment before answering.

'I see what you mean.'

'You give your young Amy a chance, along with the rest of us. After a while, God willing, you'll wonder what it was all about, especially when the kids come along.'

After that we sat for some time in silence

finishing off the bottle. Then Jack got up and walked out to the packing bay. Taking down the rope he undid the noose, coiled the rope, and hung it on the usual hook as if he had been tidying up after a day's packing.

I'm not saying that the Christmas spirit and Dad's blunt talking solved his problem, but it was enough to make him consider the options. Later, we left the empty whisky bottle and three mugs on the desk and returned to the bungalow. We went back into the house singing our own rendition of 'Silent night'. We made the excuse we had been talking family business.

I knew that I'd have to tell Jack's mum the truth; she was looking at me suspiciously.

'Well you missed a bloody good laugh on TV.'

This year the family, now including Jack and Amy's noisy three-year-old twins, will again be staying with us. So I expect it will be another traditional visit to the packing shed for some single malt Christmas spirit, followed by carols.

**About the author**
Derek Corbett retired from the Petrochemical Industry as an Engineer in 2004. Having had a story (*Natural Recycle*) included in an anthology published by Bridge House Publishing in 2015, and some success at Writing club level, he decided to see how his writing, that started as a hobby in 1984, would be received when attempting to get it published.

# The Bangkok Bash

## Robin Wrigley

### *Mulled wine*

'Patpong Road Mr Gary or straight home?' My driver Noi seemed to know my habits better than me these days.

'No, thanks, Noi. I reckon I've had enough for one night. Straight home and put your foot down.' Normally I would have gone down to Patpong to one of the many bars there.

But it was December the 23$^{rd}$ and the night of our staff Christmas party at the Australian Embassy. The Poms pride themselves on being able to do the pageantry bit but I reckon we put on the best Christmas bash amongst the embassies here. You would think the Yanks would outdo us, but they had become a bit too nervous about recent terrorist scares to put on too big a splash or invite outsiders.

Noi pulled out into the usual busy, night-time traffic and I prepared myself for a little snooze on the way home. I lived a fair way up Sukumvit Road, not far as the crow flies, but at least half an hour in this traffic.

'Good party Mr Gary? Noi asked into his rear-view mirror.

'Sure was, Noi. That's why I think it would be better to go straight home as I expect Lek will be more than a little pissed off that I'm this late, especially as she didn't come to the party.'

Lek was my regular girlfriend. We had been going steady for a while now. She worked in the Central Department Store; we met one Saturday when I was shopping there. She was a super girl but a bit out of her depth when it came to social occasions at the embassy. For that reason I decided to go on my own, which didn't go down too well.

I flopped back into the air-conditioned comfort of the car and looked out of the side window. The next thing I knew Noi was tapping me on the arm.

'Jesus, what time is it? I must have died.'

'It's two-thirty, Mr Gary, traffic was okay tonight, only take bit over half an hour.'

The house was in complete darkness which was very odd seeing as Lek was staying over and if for some reason she wasn't, the maid would have left the outside lights on before she left.

'Must be a power failure?'

'No sir,' Noi said, 'Look, house next door still got lights on.'

He was right, their lights were on alright but my compound was in complete darkness.

I'd just got out of the car and trying to adjust my vision when all of a sudden a figure loomed out of the shadows gabbling on in Thai. To my relief it was only the watchman.

'Jesus, Suporn, you scared the shit out of me!

What the bloody hell are you doing skulking about in the shadows, and why are the lights off?' These conversations happen regularly which was totally stupid on my part as neither of us understood a word spoken between us. It required Noi to take on the role of translator as well as diplomat to calm me down as my temper got the better of me.

'He say sorry, Mr Gary, he doesn't know why there's no lights. Maybe Miss Lek turned them off by mistake. He also say he sorry he frightened you but batteries in his flashlight have finished. He say he told you yesterday.'

'Alright, alright, I'll sort it out. You bugger off home, Noi. Come back at ten, I want to do a bit of shopping as I think some extra Christmas presents might be needed.'

'Okay, sir, goodnight,' with that he was off.

Gingerly I felt my way along the path from the drive to the front door. My eyes had adjusted themselves a little by now as I reached the front door, felt for the keyhole and unlocked it.

I quietly stepped inside and shut the door behind me. Once inside it seemed even darker and I cursed as I banged my shin on something heavy as I struggled to find the light switch. Recovering my balance I found them and turned them on, then as I bent down to take my shoes off, a figure leapt out of the shadow of the book case and jumped on me. For the second time in a matter of minutes I was scared out of wits until I realised from the perfume, that it was Lek.

'What the bloody hell are you doing you silly cow?'

I did my best to shake her off but it is very difficult to defend oneself without hurting her. Consequently she scratched my right cheek before I could grab her wrists.

'You are bad, bad man Gary,' she screamed in my ear as the pair of us fell to the floor. 'Why you leave me at home? Are you ashamed of me? What have I done? Have you been with some bar girl? My momma say you are butterfly.'

She was completely hysterical; I'd never seen her like this before.

'Look, I'll let you go if you can just control yourself,' I yelled. By now I was on my knees holding her by the wrists, she was half lying in front of me.

I started to get up and let go of her but she renewed her attack and flew at me again. Dodging her flailing hands, I grappled her to the ground again. I could taste the blood trickling down my cheek. With the shock and the amount of Christmas grog inside me, I was close to throwing up and would if this went on much longer.

Through the fog of alcohol I had an inspiration. God knows why I suddenly thought of it. When I was a kid visiting my granddad's farm, his old cockerel attacked me. The second time it happened, granddad was watching and he simply grabbed it by the legs, whirled it round and round above his head and tossed it into the corner of the yard. The bird tried to stand up but fell over twice before it made off looking very sorry for itself.

'That's how you deal with a stroppy chook, young feller, and works every time.' I never forgot the lesson.

That's what I needed to do to calm Lek down. I grabbed her ankles, got to my feet and started to whirl her around. This'll do the trick if nothing does.

'Garree…' she screamed, 'Put me down please.'

But I kept on spinning, just like granddad did with the cockerel. On about the second rotation I got a bit giddy and almost dropped her and then there was a sickening thud. Her head must have banged against the heavy book case. The pair of us crashed to the floor again.

'Oh Jesus! I've killed her, I've bloody killed her.'

She just lay there completely lifeless. There was a cut on her forehead and a trickle of blood was oozing from it. I could see tomorrow's headlines in the Bangkok Post – 'Australian diplomat kills Thai beauty.' This could be the end of my bloody career. Everything I'd worked for. It would be the worst scandal the embassy had ever faced. I'd be lucky if they gave me life. More likely, it would be execution by firing squad.

What a stupid, stupid bastard, what have I done? In an attempt to calm myself I tried to think as rationally as possible what to do next. I needed to get her out of here and quick. I straightened out the rug that had become rucked up, dragged her by the ankles alongside it and rolled her up in it.

Now to get her to the car and dump her somewhere, my mind was racing. Of course that silly bugger Suporn will be hanging around out there, just when I don't want him to be. I'll need to get rid of him while I put her in the boot.

I opened the door and went outside, closing it behind me.

'Suporn,' I yelled into the yard and he appeared out of the shadows but this time I was prepared and the outside lights were on anyway. I gave him a thousand Baht note and ordered, 'Beer Singha, Beer Singha, nung carton.' I made the shape of a box with my arms.

He looked at me as though I was mad. He had undertaken this simple task many times before, but perhaps never at three in the morning.

'Go on you dopey sod, get me beer.' He took the money and headed for the gates. Once he was gone I quickly opened the boot of the car. Thank God, it was empty, need to move fast.

I rushed back into the house and with a supreme effort hoisted the wrapped-up body over my shoulder. Thank goodness Thais are so light. I couldn't imagine being able to do this with one of the Sheila's back home. I staggered through the front door, put the bundle into the boot and closed the lid.

I leaned against the side of the car to catch my breath. I looked in the glove compartment for the car keys where Noi always left them, no sooner had I found them bloody Suporn was back lugging a case of beer and a grin on his face like a fox eating chicken guts in long grass.

I couldn't believe it. If I'd been dying for a beer he would have been gone for hours. I just stood staring at him. He motioned with his chin, should he carry the beer into the house. I shook my head. He mustn't see the mess inside. Because I didn't want the beer in the house he supposed I wanted it in the car and started moving towards the boot. I overtook him and tried to wrestle the case from him, but the stupid sod resisted in some dumb servile desire to complete his task.

While all this was going on I felt I was within a hair's breadth of heart failure or throwing up, or both. Then a dull thudding sound came from the boot of the car, followed by Lek's muffled cries, clearly audible in the still of the night.

'Help! Help! Someone help, please.'

We were married three weeks later in a church in Convent Road. My parents and sister came up from

Brisbane and the whole embassy turned out. We would have got married on New Year's Day but we had to wait until the bruise on Lek's forehead faded a bit.

**About the author**
Robin was a late-comer to writing fiction having joined a local writers' group in his early seventies. He has spent most of his adult life in foreign countries, over twenty in all, initially as a land surveyor and later in the geophysical exploration for oil. His experiences have given him a wealth of potential stories. However, transposing thoughts to the written word and the qwerty keyboard have now replaced the hazards he encountered in hostile environments.

# The Janus Stone

## Paula R C Readman

### *Whisky Mac on the rocks*

'It's that age old question,' my wife said turning an accusing eye in my direction as we stood staring at a stone circle high up on the wind swept moorlands.

As far as I was concerned, it was of no importance to me to find the answer to riddle of the sentinels.

'That's the trouble with you, Janus you're so blinkered, when the facts are before your very eyes.'

I cast my eyes toward the heavens and held my breath and my tongue, knowing there was no point in arguing with her. She was like a starving wolf, once she has a bone between her teeth.

'There you go, you can't deny it now. The truth hurts,' she said bitterness edging her tone.

I gave her a sideways glance; suddenly realizing she wasn't talking about the stones at all.

'Too busy looking back, aren't you?' she said, with an air of smugness.

Oh yes, she was right there. I've been accused of being backwards looking before, but I do often look forward too. Dreams of a peaceful life seemed impossible from where I was standing.

'Well, haven't you got something to say for yourself?' she snapped.

I narrowed my eyes, and wondered if it was possible.

'Oh yes, just like your father as your mother use to say, you've no balls. Well, it's about time you manned up.'

I shrugged, turned, and walked away.

'Where the hell do you think you're going Janus Lot?'

As I drove out of the car park, I did look back. My wife stood rigid with anger and disbelief that I was finally leaving her. I laughed. Not quite a pillar of salt, but close enough to leave a nasty taste in her nagging mouth.

**About the author**

Bridge House, Chapeltown, English Heritage, and Parthian Books have published Paula R C Readman's short stories. She was also the overall winner in the Writing Magazine Harrogate Crime Short Story Competition 2012.

Check out her Blog: paulareadman1.wordpress.com

Facebook: paula.readman.1@facebook.com

# Bone Collectors

## Wendy Ogilvie

### *Espresso with a shot of Sambuca*

Dante sighed as he watched his best friend walk away. He knew it was only a matter of time before Leon gave in to Skeleton. He was the leader of the Bone Collectors: a street gang who ran the south side of town. They had tried to persuade Dante to join but his grandma would kill him. Leon didn't have a grandma or a mother. His guardian was a father who drank and was too handy with his fists. Living in Barron Heights was tough for most kids; the kind of tough that steals your youth and leaves you vulnerable. Dante's mother and grandma did their best to protect him but he needed to belong, to be part of a family, and that was the pull of the Bones Collectors.

Dante turned back to go indoors and saw his grandma standing in the doorway. Her brown eyes wide as she watched Leon walking towards the old skate park. She placed one hand on her heart and held a kitchen cloth to her forehead with the other.

'Baron Samedi,' she whispered to herself.

'What's up Grandma?'

'Oh my Lord,' she said, panting heavily, 'I just seen death on the boy.'

Dante wrinkled his nose and shrugged his shoulders. 'Grandma you trippin'.'

The old woman pulled her sleeves up her chubby arms and ushered Dante up to the porch and behind the bar-covered front door. Once safely inside she stooped down and grabbed his shoulders tight.

'You listen to me child; you cannot see Leon anymore you hear me?'

Dante looked into her eyes, they were wild and scary. 'But, he's my friend.'

'That boy is mixed up with some bad people. Your mamma will have a fit if I tell her what I seen.'

'But Gran you always say things like this around Halloween. Maybe we should help Leon?'

'It's too late child. Leon is being followed by somethin' evil. You need to keep away.'

Dante screwed up his face and glanced out the window. He couldn't see anything following Leon. Grandma wasn't a fan of Halloween, she was born in Louisiana where they practiced Vodou and didn't see the need to have a special day to celebrate everything evil.

'But Mum said she was going to take us trick or treatin' tomorrow.'

'Listen to me good. Death was hovering above that boy today and I don't want you anywhere near him, you promise me now, Dante!'

Dante stepped back from her as he slowly nodded without taking his eyes off hers. She relaxed and wiped the beads of sweat from her head.

'Whatever that boy has got himself into, it's too late for him now.'

It was three hours later when Dante got the call from his mother; she had been working in the local supermarket and heard the sirens. Leon was found dead on the opposite side of the road. He had been shot in the head. A rival gang member had driven past and recognised his white bandana as Bone Collector gang colours. The police had arrested the shooter who had told them it was payback for what the Bone Collectors had done to his little brother last month. One dead boy for another.

Dante was inconsolable and cried for hours alone in his room. He didn't want to see or talk to anyone.

When the phone rang on his side table, he couldn't see the caller ID through the tears.

'Hello.'

'Dante, help me, they keep grabbing me, *help me!*'

Dante stared at his phone, 'Leon?'

'I'm sorry, it's not my fault. Please find me. It's so hot I'm burning.'

'Leon where are you?' Dante said, looking towards the window. The darkness was creeping in like next door's black cat.

'I don't know where I am,' said the voice on the phone 'but they keep grabbing me and won't let me come home.'

'I'll get my ma, she can help. Tell me where you are!'

'No she can't, it's you Dante, only you. I'm sorry, so sorry.'

Dante shivered and pulled his jacket around his shoulders.

'Wait, Leon, I'm getting Ma, she'll know what to do.'

'Just you Dante, please find me.'

'I don't know where to look.'

They're coming for you Dante, it was my only choice. I'm so sorry.'

The line went dead.

Dante pulled on his backpack, grabbed the torch from his drawer and crept into the hallway. A few of the neighbours had come in to console Leon's father who had been at their house since hearing the news. Dante had never seen him sober before. Granma was against alcohol and was busy in the kitchen making tea for everyone. He slowly unlocked the front door and slipped out.

Not knowing where to start looking, he gazed around until his eyes landed on the distant lights from the supermarket where Leon had been killed. He had never been there in the dark before; he wasn't allowed out after 7.00 p.m. It was now past eight.

Standing in front of the supermarket, Dante looked across the road. He leaned forward peering towards the road and could just make out a half visible black cat sitting between the stripes of the crossing. Slowly, heart pumping, he stepped towards the cat who stood and looked at him before walking in the direction of the skate park. Dante looked towards the park then back at the cat. He remembered being told in a story at school once that black cats were really the spirit of people who had died.

*Of course!* he thought, *the cat is has been sent by Leon to help me. The skate park was his favourite place when we were ten and skateboarding was our life.*

Dante followed the cat to the park and through the gates. The park was a large open space surrounded by bushes and tall trees. An autumn mist had descended, and the only light came from an old street lamp off to the right, its weak rays penetrating through leafless trees, casting shadows onto the concrete. There was a playground near the entrance with one working swing, a seesaw and rusty monkey bars. The skate bowl was surrounded by floodlights but they had been broken long ago.

Dante was desperate to see his friend Leon. He caught something moving to the right of him and watched as the cat slinked away through a hole in the fence. He wondered if he should follow it but he heard a scratching sound coming from under his feet. He looked down. The scratching stopped. He stood still and tried to hear over the sound of his heart thudding in his ears. The scratching noise started up again and was joined by a burrowing behind him in the grass. Dante jerked his head around to see if there was anything there. The burrowing stopped. He tried to move away but his feet were welded to the ground. Then came the scratching sound again. His body stiffened in response. *What's happening? Why can't I move?*

The sound of quick shallow breaths accompanied the continuous thud of his heart; Dante began to sway his head light, his legs heavy. His eyes darted on the ground around his feet. There it was again; he could feel the burrowing of the earth. The movement rippled nearer to his feet.

Dante let out a cry as a hand reached through the turf and grabbed his right foot. He screamed again and yanked his foot hard. His trainer slipped off and he ran as fast as he could towards the gate.

Turning briefly to make sure he wasn't being followed, he could see a black shadow with a white face emerging from the ground, pushing itself up. In his rush to find Leon, he had not processed his last words to him... *'they're coming for you, Dante.'*

With a renewed energy, he ran across the grass, his sock attaching itself to several twigs making it painful to run. He made his way to the playground and grabbed a section of the monkey bars to steady himself as his body swung around towards the park exit. He could see the gate and the street lamps ahead but now he could feel something above him. He dared not look straight up but swung his hands over his head to bat away whatever was there. His hands didn't touch anything. Whatever was hovering over him was more like a shadow or chimney smoke. He had to get away.

His right foot was now bleeding through his sock but there was no time to stop. The gate was just fifteen feet away but as he got nearer, the blackness above him extended its ebony fingers towards his face gently stroking his right cheek. The softness of its touch sent an electric bolt through his entire body.

'Get off me! Help me, somebody, help me!'

The gate was so close, Dante kept running.

On reaching the gate, he swung it open and as he looked back into the park he could see the white skeletal face of the shadow figure standing – watching. Dante held his gaze for a second or two before taking a deep breath, slamming the gate behind him and running towards his house. His throat sore and his breathing heavy – there was no time to scream for help again, he had to get home. He heaved his backpack more securely onto his shoulders, wishing he could throw it off but there wasn't time. His foot was now bleeding badly and the pain was slowing his pace but he managed to hop the last hundred yards to his front porch.

Once at his house, Dante briefly looked up before bending forward to catch his breath. The shadow above him had gone.

'What on earth happened to you boy?' His grandma asked as she walked onto the porch her hands firmly on her hips.

'I'm sorry Grandma but Leon called me. He said he needed me but there was… I saw…'

'What you talkin' about child?'

'Leon said he was sorry but he had to tell them and he didn't know where he was.'

Dante's grandma dropped her shoulders and moved towards him. 'What did he tell them; what did you do?'

'Nothing, it wasn't me Gran. I was trying to stop Leon but…' Dante's eyes filled with tears and his body began to shudder as he struggled to get his words out.'

His grandma took a few steps back from him, put her hands on his arm and looked into his eyes. 'Did Leon kill that little boy?'

Dante looked at the floor and wiped his nose on his sleeve. 'He didn't mean to. They made him do it.'

'Were you there? – *Dante!* Were you with Leon?'

Dante slowly lifted his head to look at her but she didn't look back at him; she was staring at something just above his head.

**About the author**
Wendy has been a Personal Trainer for twenty years but has always made time for writing; She is currently editing the sequel to her Chick Lit novel *Wandering on the Treadmill* and completing her first thriller.

https://wendyogilvie.wordpress.com

# Harry's Going to Die Anyway
## Robin Wrigley

### *Campari & Ruby Red Grapefruit Juice*

The only time I met Ismail he was crouched down against the rough brick and flint church wall at the bus stop at St Mark's church where I had been cleaning the altar brasses.

'Are you alright?' My question was rather rhetorical as he certainly looked unwell if not odd crouched down there in this cold weather now threatening to rain or snow.

'Harry's going to die anyway,' he muttered fleetingly glancing in my direction and then back at the pavement.

'Who is Harry? And even if he is there is no point in you joining him which you certainly will if you continue sitting down there in this weather young man. Here, let me help you up.'

He attempted to avoid my help by moving his elbow into his side but I kept a firm hold and he allowed me to bring him up to a standing position. I was quite surprised when seeing him face to face how young he was and that he was an inch or two shorter than me. His face was a light milky-tea brown, with the pubescent, wispy-makings of a beard. His hair was simply black, long and unkempt. If I hadn't discovered him cooping there on a winter's afternoon I would have assumed he had just got out of bed having spent the night fully clothed in his current attire.

'What's your name?'

'Ismail. What do you want with me missus? I wan't doin' any harm wuz I? I always get down like that when dis cold wind is blowin'. Ain't no law about that is there?' He looked so desperate, so helpless, yet so hopeless part of me wanted to shake him while the other half wanted to hug him but I resisted.

His nose started to run but before I could fish for a tissue from my bag he had wiped it away on the sleeve of his combat jacket that showed signs of previous similar use.

'So, tell me who is this friend Harry and why is he going to die?'

'It's a long story missus and I ain't got time to tell you. You can't help him. Nobody can help him so just forget it. You got any money you can spare me?'

How many times had my brother told me not to give in these situations. Don't take out you purse and let them see it. But I did. I took my purse from my bag, opened it – there was a ten and a twenty pound note inside. I hesitated then gave him both.

'There, that's all I have I'm afraid but it should buy you something hot. Where will you go now you're on your own?'

His face almost broke into a smile but not quite.

He took the money politely and crumpled the notes into a grubby hand touching his heart all in one movement.

'Fanks missus, don't you worry about me, somemink will come up, really.'

He turned and shuffled off down St Mark's Avenue just as the street lights came on. I stood and watched him until his pathetic figure disappeared over the crest of the avenue. I brushed a tear from my cheek unsure if it was from sorrow or the cold December wind that was starting to pick up; turned around and headed for home.

The following morning I called the local police station and asked if there had been any accidents the previous day. They said a young Asian boy had been fatally wounded in a hit and run accident. He didn't have any identity papers on him and had no idea if his name was Harry. They were curious as to why I wanted to know as he had a large letter 'H' tattooed on the back of his hand.

**About the author**
Robin was a late-comer to writing fiction having joined a local writers' group in his early seventies. He has spent most of his adult life in foreign countries, over twenty in all, initially as a land surveyor and later in the geophysical exploration for oil. His experiences have given him a wealth of potential stories. However, transposing thoughts to the written word and the qwerty keyboard have now replaced the hazards he encountered in hostile environments.

# A Bridge Over Troubled Waters
## Robin Wrigley

### *A bottle of still mineral water*

As I turned the corner and climbed the pavement leading up to the bridge over the river, a figure caught my eye. Though my mind was on other matters, I instantly recognised the young waitress who only a couple of hours before had served my lunch in the hotel restaurant.

I could have sworn she was attempting to hoist herself onto the bridge wall but stopped when she saw me, dropped back to the pavement and just stared ahead along the river.

'Hello – are you okay?' I ventured unsure if I should intervene, worried I could be wrong and my approach rebuked.

'I'm okay thanks – you startled me that's all.' She glanced briefly in my direction before turning back to the river. I think I caught a hint of an eastern European accent but I couldn't be sure as she spoke so softly.

She was slight with blonde hair fashioned in a pony-tail just as she was in the restaurant. No longer wearing her uniform she was dressed in jeans and a faded red hoodie. The strangest thing was she did not have any shoes on, odd in mid-October.

'Are you sure? It looked to me as though you

were trying to climb on to the wall. Where on earth are your shoes? Aren't your feet cold?

'Really I'm okay – please leave me alone – please.' She wasn't rude just sad and pleading. I was tempted to acquiesce but something said I should persist.

'Look I'm sorry if you think I'm being nosey but I think if we got off this bridge and had a chat I might be of some help.'

This last remark seemed as though it sliced through her control and she sank to a crouch position rather like a marionette would collapse when the puppeteer drops the strings. She clutched her face in her hands and muttered through them, 'Why couldn't you just leave me alone?'

'I suppose I could but I'm sure you've noticed I am a priest and I apologise for interfering; you see I am obliged to offer help even when as it appears, it is not welcome. Come, I'm sure we can find some solution to your problems.' By now I was beginning to worry how this might appear to a passer-by but thankfully the place was quite quiet.

As circumstances stood my thoughts were as much for myself as for this poor unfortunate young woman and in all honesty it might be better if we linked hands and jumped together. I quickly banished the thought.

I was on my way to an interview with the Bishop that could well spell the end of my career. The misinterpretation of this situation with a young girl crouched as if in fear of me could easily tip the balance of the scales of my future, already in serious jeopardy.

'Get off her you bastard!' I turned just in time to receive a painful blow to my left jaw that sent me sprawling over the crouching girl onto the pavement beyond her, catching my elbow against the stone wall and knocking off my glasses.

My assailant, as far as I could make out without my glasses, had a bushy beard and was wearing black and white check trousers the sort favoured by professional chefs.

'Come on Alicia let's get away from this pervert. As for you mate you ain't 'eard the last of this.'

Before I could say a word they were gone, I was abandoned on the pavement searching for my glasses.

**About the author**
Robin was a late-comer to writing fiction having joined a local writers' group in his early seventies. He has spent most of his adult life in foreign countries, over twenty in all, initially as a land surveyor and later in the geophysical exploration for oil. His experiences have given him a wealth of potential stories. However, transposing thoughts to the written word and the qwerty keyboard have now replaced the hazards he encountered in hostile environments.

# It's Never the Same
## Paula R C Readman

### *Farmhouse Scrumpy*

It's amazing just how much mess a shotgun makes. It's not as though I wasn't aware of how dangerous they can be in the wrong hands. Growing up on a farm as I did, my father made sure I was more than capable of handling one.

'Don't ever leave a loaded gun just lying around, Gwen,' he said as Mum nervously watched on. His big, strong, gentle hands took the gun from mine, and replaced it, where it always hung on the wall in the kitchen.

I was 14 years old, when Mum passed away. There had only ever been the three of us, though I never felt my father regretted not having a son. I guess he saw me as being just as capable of doing the same work as a boy could, especially with his guidance.

Dad used to take me shooting with him, so I've seen the damage a gun can do to an animal or a bird, but somehow it isn't the same as shooting a man close up, I can assure you. Though having said that, it isn't the same as it is portrayed on the telly either.

As I stand here, looking down at this poor excuse of a man, I wish it were just a fictional crime programme, where everything is rather sterile. I could do with a flashback, or even better still, a flash forward. It would be handy knowing how it's all going to end for me. Maybe, if I'd held my temper, seen a little less red, things might've turned out different for me, and especially for him. I wish my dear old dad had seen fit to warn me about lying, cheating bastards.

The shotgun was the first thing that came to hand when that old red mist descended. When you're on your own in an old farmhouse on the moors, you need to be careful, especially at night. There's been too many thefts of expensive farm equipment in the area. Well, that's the story I'll be sticking to when the police arrive.

If only he'd listened to me. None of this would've happened. I didn't see why I should have listen to anymore of his lies. I couldn't stand seeing what was happening to all my father's hard work as he drunk our livelihood away. It's amazing how resourceful a desperate woman can be when she wants to be. With a little spring cleaning everything will be as good as new.

Aha, that sounds like them now. Breathe easy. Remember look distraught. Bearing in mind how easy it was the last time.

**About the author**
Bridge House, Chapeltown, English Heritage, amd Parthian Books have published Paula R C Readman's short stories. She was also the overall winner in the Writing Magazine Harrogate Crime Short Story Competition 2012.

Check out her Blog: paulareadman1.wordpress.com

Facebook: paula.readman.1@facebook.com

# Down By the River

## Ann Dixon

### *Sparkling water*

With all her household chores finished Enid Fisher danced her way to her secret hideaway down by the River Clare. Amidst its many twists and turns was a small inlet, hidden from the view of prying eyes by the long delicate fronds of a Weeping Willow tree. From the land, it was hidden by a wide stretch of Blue Elderberry shrubs and a mass of tangled Juniper bushes. With a bit of luck thought Enid, Harry would be waiting for her. She had thought long and hard before inviting him to the hideaway, but Harry had proved to be a stalwart friend and had even taken on Jem Galloway, the school bully, when he had tried to steal her school bag. To be absolutely sure though, she had insisted he take a blood oath, swearing never to reveal its location to anyone – especially grown-ups.

Enid twirled and hummed as she drank in the fresh, sweet, smell of summer. and ahead of her, the River Clare twinkled mischievously in the sunlight. As she got closer Enid looked around to make sure no one was following her, or could see where she would duck into the swirl of Juniper branches. All was clear – the only onlookers, a few stray cows meandering on Darrow Head.

'Where have you been ?' asked Harry, as Enid emerged into the dappled light. 'I've been waiting for ages. I thought you might have forgotten.'

'Harry Dempster! You do talk a lot of tommyrot. I know you had to muck out the pigs this morning and that's at least an hour's job. Besides, you know I can't get away before all my chores are finished. Aunt Gwyneth insists on checking everything I do before I'm allowed out. Anyone would think I was a servant rather than her niece.' Enid slumped to the ground and lay back on the grassy bank.

'Let's not argue,' said Harry. 'Look! I've set up my fishing rod, just liked you asked. If we're lucky we might catch a whale or two.'

Enid laughed, sat up and joined Harry by the riverbank.

The minutes ticked by and the line remained languid and still.

'I don't think there are any fishes in this river, let alone whales,' moaned Enid. 'I've been sitting here for ages. This is boring.'

'Fishing takes patience,' replied Harry, 'and clearly you ain't got very much.'

Enid stuck out her tongue and was just about to throw down the rod in disgust when there was a sudden pull on the line.

'Hey! Harry, I think I've got something. Come and help. I think I might have caught a whale after all.'

It took Enid and Harry almost ten minutes to land their whale, which turned out in the end to be a monster sized carp.

'A whale, a whale, I've caught a whale,' he whooped.

'Let me hold him then,' said Enid excitedly.

He placed the carp in Enid's hands, and as he did so she leant over and kissed him, firmly on the lips.

'Wow!' said Harry, and returned her kiss with equal ardour. A cheeky grin spread across his nut brown face. 'If that's my reward for helping you catch a whale I think I'll catch another?'

Enid blushed.

'Now don't you go getting any ideas Harry Dempster,' she replied. 'I'm not that sort of girl.' Harry winked at her.

'As if I would. I'm a knight in shining armour I am, a veritable Sir Lancelot. Chivalry's my middle name.' Harry bowed low and within minutes they were both in fits of laughter.

'I think we'd better return our whale to his watery home,' said Harry.

Together they bent down and replaced the carp in the river.

'Goodbye Tommy Whale,' whispered Enid. 'KEEP SAFE!' The carp flipped its tail and swiftly darted away to the safety of deeper water.

For a few moments they stood looking nervously at each other. Enid was the first to break the awkward silence.

'Thanks for teaching me how to fish,' she said quietly.

'And thanks for that kiss,' said Harry. 'I must admit, it was a bit of a surprise. Does this mean you actually like me Enid Fisher?'

'Course it does you ninny. Otherwise I wouldn't have told you about this place.'

Harry reached over to Enid and swung her round. 'Then from now on you're my girl,' he said.

The sun began to set over Darrow Head and Enid and Harry said their farewells. 'Same time tomorrow?' asked Harry hopefully.

'Why yes, dear sir,' replied Enid. 'I do believe I have a space in my busy diary,' and together they walked to the top of the hill hand in hand. Many more assignations followed over the years and in 1913 Harry and Enid married.

Their bliss was unfortunately short lived. Harry joined the army at the outbreak of the War and for five years its monstrous shadow blocked out the sunshine of their love.

When Harry returned to Blighty he was not the same man that Enid had married. He had become quiet and introvert. The lively, outgoing, happy go lucky man she knew, was locked away in a distant land of memories that he would not -or could not share.

Enid so much wanted to help Harry but he resolutely refused to talk about his war experiences. She surmised that the memories were just too painful.

One morning when Enid was cleaning out the cupboard under the stairs, she came across their fishing rods which had fallen behind some wooden shelving. Her thoughts immediately ran back to those early days when she and Harry would meet in their secret hideaway down by the river. She smiled to herself as she recalled the day that she first kissed him. His expression had been one of complete surprise and also of absolute joy. From that day, all those years ago she knew that they were meant for each other.

Enid was about to replace the rods when a sudden idea popped into her head. 'Hey! Harry. You'll never guess what I've just found.'

'You mean you've actually found something in that cupboard? It's like the black hole of Calcutta under there.'

'Well! I've just found these,' said Enid extracting the rods. 'How about we brush them off, grab some bait, and go fishing?'

'I don't know about that,' replied Harry doubtfully. 'It's been a long time, love, and I've probably lost the knack after all these years.'

'Well ! Harry Dempster, you'll never know until you try,' said Enid resolutely. 'I know just the place down by the River Clare?' Harry laughed. 'Come on Harry, just for old time's sake.'

Harry looked across at Enid's smiling face. How could he say no.

That afternoon, the two of them pushed their way past the juniper bushes and emerged into their secret river bank world.

'Come on then Harry. Let's get cracking!' said Enid encouragingly.

'I will,' said Harry, 'but not before you give me a kiss. No kiss means no whales and we can't have that, can we?'

Enid eagerly complied. The kiss was long and tender.

Two hours later Harry was happily chattering away and Enid caught a heart-tingling glimpse of the man she had married all those years ago.

That day, fishing by the river, was to be the first of many. They were days when Harry could free his troubled mind and focus on the beauty of nature. His battle was not now with a fierce some enemy but with an array of clever and intelligent fish. On those days that Enid and Harry fished together, he would smile and talk joyously about their carefree, childhood.

So it was, that gradually, day by day, week by week and month by month, Harry Dempster slowly recovered. Harry would always say that he put his recovery down to the love of a good woman and the quiet search for Tommy, the riverbank whale.

On one particular summer morning, as he waited patiently by the riverbank for the fish to bite, he took out his pen knife and carved a heart in the bark of the Willow Tree. Underneath it read – Harry loves Enid 1926 He stepped back to admire his handy work.

'Oh dear,' he said after a while. 'I do believe I've forgotten someone.' He returned to the tree and added the following: **Harry loves Enid 1926 and Tommy – our whale.**

**About the author**
Ann is a retired primary school teacher and has written many short stories in a range of genres. She has also written a fantasy fiction book for children entitled *The Bewitching of Esme Smart*. She hopes to publish this sometime next year.

# Postcard Lady

## Keith Havers

### *Whisky chaser*

I was staring across the sand as I ambled along the parade. Although the weather was fine, it was early in the season and the beach was almost deserted. A young couple were attempting to fly a kite for the benefit of their two children. The youngsters looked indifferent as they sat huddled together in their twin buggy. Two elderly women were inspecting a pool of water which had collected in one of the depressions in the sand by the breakwater.

The group which caught my attention was three teenagers and an older woman, presumably their mum. They were playing that French game, similar to our bowls, except you lob the ball instead of rolling it. Boules, I believe it's called. Mum was a woman of, I think the polite term is 'ample proportions'. She reminded me of those red-faced women on the comic postcards I had just been browsing down in the seafront café.

I stopped near one of those Victorian promenade shelters. The ones with a roof and slatted benches which face all four points of the compass. The boys had all loosened off a couple of shots but I could see they each still had another ball -sorry, boule -remaining. At this point mum decided to walk out to the Jack or whatever it's called in this game (le Jacques?) and take a closer look at the lie of the boules. The thought occurred to me that, when I was about those kids' age, it would be too big a temptation to resist, seeing my mum enter the target area. I wouldn't have intended any harm, of course, but a mischievous lob in her vicinity would have been enough to satisfy my impish sense of humour. With her back towards her offspring she bent down to get a closer look. That was tempting fate even further I thought.

Just then I spotted a man coming along the prom towards me. He had also witnessed the scene and was obviously of the same opinion as myself. Unfortunately he couldn't resist making his thoughts known and he shouted out over the parapet.

'Dun't bend over luv! It's too big a target! Yow'll mek it too easy for 'em!'

He looked at me and winked.

'She'll need to do a boil wash tomorrow!' he added.

I chuckled at his rustic drollness and returned my attention to the family. The wind must have been offshore because his rude jibes had clearly carried and, unsurprisingly, they had not been appreciated. The two bigger lads had begun running up the beach towards us followed by mum, who was amazingly agile for one so plump. I remember observing that those boys were older and bigger than I first thought and they looked as if they meant business. I turned back to the man to gauge his reaction but he had disappeared. I then realised that he had ducked behind the shelter. It occurred to me that this was not an ideal hiding place and that he would shortly be discovered. It soon became apparent, however, that I had not fully grasped the situation. The three irate group members were still calling and pointing up towards me. Then it dawned. They believed me to be the guy with the wisecracks. At first I wasn't too alarmed. Surely I could explain the situation and all would be resolved. Then I took another look at their bearing and considered the options of discretion and valour. Prudence vastly outweighed courage and so a hasty retreat was called for.

I sprinted along the prom, back the way I came. This was my first mistake as I had to run past the steps which led up from the beach. The first youth was already halfway up as I ran past the top. I'm not a young man and have never been very athletic but it is surprising what you can achieve when the suggestion of a severe beating is likely. I glanced over my shoulder to see the pair emerge from behind the seawall. I was heartened to see that there was a fair distance between us. My next problem, though, was 'Where do I go from here?'.

By now I had reached the recreation area where gardens and fountains vied with putting greens and other leisure activities. Reasoning that they couldn't do me much harm in front of witnesses, I decided to try to lose my pursuers amongst the other holiday makers. I skipped behind a hedge and found myself alongside the municipal bowling green where several games were going on. I ran along the path which bordered the playing area, trying to avoid the onlookers and casual observers. When I had reached the halfway mark I looked ahead and realised to my horror that one of the youths had managed to circle round and get ahead of me. He was waiting at the end of the path. I stopped and turned around to see his brother approaching from the other direction with menace.

There was nothing else for it. I stepped smartly onto the neatly trimmed grass and made swiftly and directly for the other side. Leaping over balls and sidestepping players, I had almost reached the edge of the green when a stray Jack found its way underneath my feet and I careered straight into a bunch of elderly ladies. Picking myself up and taking a split second to check that no-one was seriously hurt I continued my escape, now chased by one or two of the bowls players. Although I felt that I was running – if not for my life – then at least for my personal safety, the irony of both Boules and Bowls players being in hot pursuit was not lost on me.

By now my body was in areas it had not been in since primary school. All available oxygen that I could draw into my gasping lungs was going in to feeding my leg muscles, thus starving my brain of the stuff essential for logical thinking. So, left to make their own decisions, my legs just carried on in a straight line. By now I was in the middle of the ornamental gardens, leaving a trail of broken stems and trampled blooms behind me. Fortunately my flailing limbs had the presence of mind to skirt around the goldfish pond. Unfortunately they hadn't allowed for any obstacle to be hidden on the other side of the low wall and hadn't the strength to hurdle the wheelbarrow which a council worker had thoughtlessly parked there. I rapped my shins on the edge of the infernal receptacle and sent it and its contents in all directions. I managed to stay on my feet, though, and kept going. One quick glimpse behind me revealed a rake-bearing gardener had now joined the posse.

Having learned nothing from their wheelbarrow experience, my legs continued their policy of 'straight ahead and damn the consequences'. My eyes, which were streaming tears and stinging from the sweat pouring down my forehead, could just about make out the Novelty Rock Emporium across the road. My diminishing powers of reasoning seemed to believe that this would be a safe haven.

There was only the Crazy Golf Course between me and sanctuary.

By now, legs had got the hang of the side-step and I negotiated my way around windmills, ramps, mushrooms and all the other paraphernalia that make up this bizarre game. As I came to the perimeter of the playing area I narrowly avoided running into a small child that had wandered across my path. Alas, this resulted in putting me on a collision course with mummy and daddy who were pushing the empty baby-buggy. I managed to spare the parents but shunted the pushchair into a miniature lighthouse.

Undaunted, I reached the pavement and fixed both eyes on my intended destination. Then the sign in the window came into focus – CLOSED. My spirits plummeted but I was too high on adrenalin to give up now. I took a sharp right back towards the beach with a whole gaggle of pursuers right behind me. My brain had gone completely couch potato now and, for some reason, the Benny Hill theme tune began running through my head. I reached the prom and saw a set of steps leading down to the beach in front of me. I plunged down three at a time and leapt the final few feet into the soft sand. I collapsed to my knees and was about to get to my feet when a pair of white trainers and black slacks appeared a few inches in front of my face. I looked up to see big momma from the Boules game standing over me. She took me by the shoulders and two huge arms hauled me upright. I tried to regain my breath but she was dusting the sand from my clothes and knocking it back out of me in the process.

'It wasn't me,' I finally gasped. 'It was another bloke. Shouting all those rude comments at you. It wasn't me. I was just looking. He shouted and then he hid. I ran because he hid and I thought you wouldn't believe me and those lads looked very angry and I didn't want any trouble. Please believe me.'

My brain was still refusing to get off its backside and it was mouth's turn to make me look a complete idiot.

'Yes, I know,' she said.

'You know?'

'Yes,' she continued. 'I found him cowering in that hut thing. I could tell it was him from his accent when he tried denying it all.'

'What did you do to him?'

'Nothing much I could do, apart from give him a fright. I don't think he'll be doing that again in a hurry.'

By now the mob had gathered around us and, after some explanation by the lady (notice how she's now gone up in status?) and some grovelling from me, all was resolved.

I strolled along the beach with the woman and her two sons, back to where they had left the youngest guarding the boules.

'I'm sensitive about my size,' the woman grumbled. 'And I hate it when people are so rude.'

'I would never dream of ridiculing another person's physical appearance,' I lied.

We reached the spot where the young man was waiting patiently. The boules were still lying where they had left them.

'I'm afraid we haven't time to finish our game, boys,' she said. 'It's time to pack up and go home.'

As she bent down to gather up the equipment there was a sharp ripping sound. I gazed around to see that the seam of her trousers had finally relinquished the effort of holding them together and allowed the two halves to part company, revealing an off-white coloured undergarment that could have doubled up as a chair cover. The five of us looked at each other in embarrassment, not knowing what to say. The man's comments about the state of tomorrow's laundry came into my head (thanks, brain – brilliant time to get off the sofa). I tried to lock the store cupboard where my laughing gear is kept but – too late. Just before the door closed, a guffaw and a couple of chortles squeezed out. I put my hand to my mouth and waited for the reaction. It looked as if I was going to get my whipping after all. There was a silence which lasted for just a few seconds but which seemed like an age and then something wonderful happened. The whole family collapsed into hysterics. All five of us were gripped in fits of laughter which rendered us helpless.

The family were still cackling away as I drifted off back to my digs. I made a mental note to give my brain a severe reprimand when we got home.

**About the author**
Keith Havers' short stories are frequently published in various popular magazines. He is a member of Trowell Writers' Club and Nottingham Writers' Club. He works as an invigilator for vocational exams at a local college. In his spare time he enjoys cycling and spending time with his two grandchildren.

https://keithhavers.wordpress.com

# Film Noir

## Gill James

### *Orange juice*

'To the side a little. That's it. Now smile. Look down.'

Snap. Snap.

Cherry's neck and shoulders ached with the effort of holding her head stiffly for so long. Despite the hot studio lights, she was trying not to shiver. She had to admit: it was just as her mother had promised. Being this thin made her feel the cold. She could hear that constant voice. 'You need to eat. You have to keep your strength up. Young girls don't need to be that slim.' The trouble was they did. Even if it made them feel cold.

'Come on sweetheart. Where's that lovely smile. Not long now.'

Snap. Snap.

'Okay, honey. That's it.'

'I have to give it to you. They look good.' They were studying the portfolio Gaston Pictures had sent through.

Cherry wasn't so sure. 'They make me look fat, Mum.'

'Don't be silly. You're not at all fat. That red top really suits you.' Her mother frowned. 'Even if it does show more than it ought to.'

'Mum!'

'Well at least they're good pictures. They ought to get you some work.'

Her mother sniffed. 'They'd really better with what they've cost.'

Cherry shuddered. Had this really been such a good idea after all? What if it didn't work? It had to. It just had to.


'Yes your portfolio was very nice, dear, but we have hundreds of collections like that. You really need to be a bit different to stand any chance these days.'

'Perhaps I should try somewhere else?'

'Well, I don't think you'll find anywhere more efficient than our company.' The receptionist glared down at Cherry from her high stool. She seemed to be turning up her nose as if Cherry was something the cat had brought in. 'Anyway, we've already gone to substantial time and trouble circulating your portfolio to the top companies. If you withdrew now we would have to charge you.'

'How much?'

The receptionist tapped her long fingernail on the keyboard. She glanced at her computer screen and smirked. 'Five hundred and seventy-five pounds.'

That was it then. She wouldn't be able to get out of this.

The receptionist smiled a little more gently now.

'You'll have to be patient. Once they've seen you enough they'll start remembering your face. You've got quite a pretty face, really.'

*It doesn't help, though, does it?* Mum was going to be furious.

'Where are you off to in such a tearing hurry?'

Oh no. It was Kevin Hughes. She'd never hear the last of it if he told everybody at school where he'd seen her.

'Aw, you've not been to one of those poncy agencies who promise to get you modelling jobs. Rip off or what?'

'Shut up, Kevin Hughes.'

'You'd do better letting me take you on my mobile and pasting it on Facebook.'

'Don't you dare.'

Snap. Too late. He'd done it. There would be trouble if he did put it on Facebook. The agency would drop her. It was a strict rule: no promoting yourself on social media.

Kevin was now already half way down the High Street.

Two weeks later when she called at the agency there was a much younger receptionist there. Candy, said her name badge. Cherry guessed she was only a couple of years older than herself.

'Hiya. Cherry isn't it? We've had a bit of news.'

Her heart started thumping and her mouth went dry. Was this going to be her big moment?

Candy tapped away at her keyboard. The printer

whirred into life and started chugging out paper.

'Modes Gaston. They'd like to actually see you. Only thing is, they want you to lose a couple of kilos. And they'd like you to have your hair cropped and streaked orange. Of course, they'd expected it done at a top salon. The details are here.' She handed Cherry the printout. 'There's a list of recommended salons at the end with a list of charges.'

Cherry looked at the papers. God, her mother was going to freak.

'Now, don't go getting your hopes up too much. You'll have to make those changes before they'll even look at you. They may still reject you. But it's a step in the right direction and cause for celebration. Go, girl.'

Kevin Hughes was waiting on the pavement again when she got outside. Before she could stop him he'd got out his phone and was snapping away.

'Please don't put them on Facebook,' she begged. 'It will spoil everything.'

Kevin grinned. 'Okay. I promise I won't Give us your phone and I'll put my number in. Then send us a text so I've got your number and I'll send the pictures over. So that you can see how much better I am than whoever you're paying all that money to.'

Cherry sighed and gave him the phone.

'Oh my god. What have they done to you?' It was the snooty older receptionist again. 'I hope you didn't pay them. In fact they ought to pay you. Compensation for wrecking your career.'

It had looked all right when they'd first got it done. No way would her mother pay those top salon prices and they'd gone to the place in the village her mother used. But now it was beginning to grow out and her dark roots were showing. Her hair had gone really dry as well. It had taken her quite a while to lose the extra two kilos.

She felt really ill. She'd not slept because she'd been so hungry.

'Listen, sweetie, we'll have to get you fixed. I'm going to make you an appointment with one of our recommended salons.'

'I don't think I can afford it,' Cherry mumbled.

'You can't afford not to. And we can't afford for you not to have this put right. We'll just take the fee out of your first pay packet. Take a seat over there.'

The woman seemed to take ages on the phone. Cherry felt really sick and thought she might have to rush out at any minute to throw up.

'There. You've an appointment in half an hour at Gregor's. There's a taxi waiting outside.'

Thank goodness she could get out now.

She rushed down the stairs. The fresh air made her feel a little better straight away. There was the taxi waiting for her. And so was Kevin.

Snap. Snap. Snap.

Why must he keep taking photos?

The flash made her blink. But when she tried to open her eyes there was just blackness.

'Oh you're awake now then?'

Cherry's head hurt. She couldn't make out where she was. Her arm was sore. There was a tube sticking into it. It led to a bag of clear fluid that was hanging off something that looked a bit like a hat stand.

'The doctors say you were dehydrated. And that you're much too thin. This lark has got to stop my girl.'

'Leave me alone, Mum.'

What was she doing here? What about Gregor's and Gaston? She guessed that would all be over for a while, if not for good.

'Okay, I'll leave you for a bit. He wants a word.'

She looked to where her mother was pointing.

Oh no. Kevin Hughes again.

'You scared us. Are you all right now?'

'What do you want, Kevin?'

He took a large brown envelope out of his shoulder bag. 'This came. I thought you might like to see it.'

'Bog off, Kevin.'

'Okay, I'm going.' He put envelope on the bedside table and held his arms up in the air.

'What did he want?' Her mother was holding a cup of what looked like dishwater but she suspected it was supposed to be weak coffee.

Cherry nodded towards he envelop.

'Aren't you going to open it?'

'Shall I?'

Her mum opened the envelop before she could even pick it up. 'Oh my god.' She put her hand in front of her mouth.

'What is it?'

Her mother handed her a large black and white photograph. It was of Cherry with her hair tousled and looking just a little bit tired. Yet there was something extraordinarily good about it. She looked, well, glamorous.

'It's fantastic, isn't it?'

Yes, it was good. But she didn't want to agree with her mother too soon.

'Oh, wait. There's something else here.' She pulled out a closely typed document.

'What is it?'

Her mother took a few moments to read it.

'Apparently you've been invited to work for the Nouveau Film Noir Company.'

'What's that?'

'They make old-fashioned black and white films. Did I leave my phone here?' Kevin was back and was now on his hands and knees searching under the bed.

'Only they want you to put on a bit of weight. Listen. Grow the orange hair out, they say. But keep the tom-boy look.' Her mum looked up from the letter. 'See. I told you.'

'You didn't mind me sending them off, did you? Only I knew you would be exactly what they were looking for.' Kevin scrambled up on to his feet, the phone now in his hand. 'The photos look really good in black and white.'

**About the author:**
Gill James writes all sorts of fiction – novels, short fiction, flash fiction and experimental fiction. She is also a publisher and editor.

Visit her blog at www.gilljameswriter.eu

# Knit and Natter

## Dawn Knox

### *Tea with lemon*

'D'you think that'll be enough?' Florrie Fanshawe asked, stabbing the air with a bony finger as she counted each of the plastic chairs she'd arranged around the village hall table.

'Mm hmm, six should be enough,' Harriet replied. 'Peggy's still got the 'flu, Doris is in Brighton and as for poor Gladys…' She crossed herself.

'Oh, yes, Gladys, poor thing. Is she still…?

'Mm hmm.'

'Oh dear.'

Florrie wiped her skeletal finger across the top of the table and inspected it. 'Just look at this!' she held out the evidence. 'Filth!' Clicking open the clasp on her handbag, she pulled out a pack of wipes and scrubbed at the pitted, wooden surface of the table. Once satisfied, she fished in her handbag again and produced a spray of air freshener from which she let out several frenzied blasts. A fragrant, lemon scent struggled bravely with the musty, fusty air in the village hall but was soon vanquished.

'What's the target now?' Harriet asked as Florrie took a pile of knitted squares from a large carrier bag and placed them in the middle of the table.

'Well, we were aiming for ten blankets but we

seem to have got through the first four quite quickly, so I'd like to suggest we increase it to a dozen. What d'you think?'

'Mm hmm. The people at the dog's home are always appealing for extra blankets, so I'd say yes. It looks like Knit and Natter is a great success. Perhaps we ought to pay for the hall for a further three months.'

'Yes, I think you're right.'

When everyone had arrived, Florrie took a notebook from her capacious handbag and listed everyone's name. 'Harriet Pettara, Edna Harbottle, Mary Wilson, Rita Gupta, Sebastian Milligrew...' she turned to the new lady, 'and you are?'

'Bella Carrossetti, two R's, two S's and two T's.'

'Rrsstt?' asked Florrie reading what she'd written.

'Well, I expected you to work out all the other letters yourself.' Bella shook her head in disbelief and the bun on top of her head wobbled precariously. 'Here,' she said taking a handful of business cards from her pocket with a perfectly manicured hand and distributed one in front of each person at the table.

'Bella's Beauty Box,' she said proudly. 'I'm the proprietor. Beauty in Basilwade or Wherever You Are,' she added. 'Ten percent off on presentation of this card.'

'Oh my!' she said as Rita reached out to take the card that had been placed in front of her. 'Don't worry, there's nothing to be ashamed of,' she added as Rita snatched her hand away, 'False nails would be perfect for you. There's not much you can do with nails that shape or in that state but I'll be able to make them look reasonable. Just give me a ring and ask for a Bella's Special Manicure.'

Rita stared at the card as if willing it to glide towards her without having to expose her hands again.

'And don't think that gentlemen aren't welcome, I have lots of male customers. It's really quite manly now to have manicures,' Bella said to Sebastian who thrust his hands in his pockets and shrank behind Edna.

'Or facials,' Bella added.

*He's rather shy,* mouthed Edna.

'He's what?' Bella asked, craning her neck to get a better look at Sebastian who checked his watch, rose apologetically, his face crimson. He mumbled something and rushed out.

Everyone looked accusingly at Bella.

'Oh my!' she said, 'He forgot his card. 'Scuse me a moment, while I chase after him—'

'No!' said the Knit and Natter ladies in unison.

Bella sat down and patted her topknot. 'I'll give it to him next week.'

'Now, if we could get on,' Florrie said, glancing sideways at Bella, nostrils flared and eyebrows drawn together. 'Well, ladies, we've almost finished blanket number five. Just three more squares needed. We've had suggestions for a colour scheme for number six. Mary would like blue and red—'

There was a sharp intake of breath from Bella.

'Oh, no! Oh my, no! Red and blue will never do,' she said in a sing-song voice.

Harriet, the peace-keeper, replaced the blue wool that Florrie had laid next to the red one with a green ball.

Bella tutted.

'Red and blue will never do. Red and green should never be seen,' Bella said.

Florrie turned to Bella and fixed her with the look that even Amy, her teenage daughter, with all the insouciance of youth, recognised as a tipping point before a cataclysmic eruption. Florrie was halfway through the inhalation that would launch the explosion when Bella leapt up.

'Stop right there! Freeze!' said Bella.

Florrie stopped and froze.

Bella pulled a pair of tweezers from her pocket and grabbed Florrie by the chin.

'There!' she said triumphantly as she applied the tweezers to Florrie's jaw and plucked.

'I've never seen such a large whisker on a woman before,' she said holding the hair still trapped between the jaws of the tweezers so that all the ladies could admire it.

'Would you like me to dab that with witch hazel? I swear by the stuff,' she asked Florrie who cradled her chin as if she'd been punched. Florrie shook her head, eyes wide with shock.

The other ladies surreptitiously probed their faces with exploratory fingers, all eyes on Bella.

'Oh my!' said Bella whose gaze had alighted on Harriet. She sprang to her feet. 'Such tension!'

Bella rolled her sleeves up and reached out as if to play the piano. Harriet gulped and her eyes swivelled in their sockets as she tried to see behind her without moving her head which was now clamped in Bella's vice-like grip. With elbows raised, she began to knead the muscles in Harriet's neck and shoulders.

'Oh my! I've never felt such locked muscles. How on earth d'you move your head?' Harriet's eyes were watering as Bella squeezed and pulled, then performed some chopping actions with the edge of her hand.

*HELP!* Mouthed Harriet. But no one dared move.

'Better?' Bella asked silkily, poking her head over Harriet's shoulder.

Harriet nodded.

She was beyond speech.

'Goodness me,' said Edna, checking her watch, 'is that the time? I really should be going.' So far, she and Mary had been the only ones to escape Bella's scrutiny.

'So soon?' said Florrie, whose tone dripped acid.

She might just as easily have said 'Sit down! If we've had to put up with these indignities, don't think you're going to get away with it!'

Edna went into the kitchen with a toss of her head and returned a few minutes later with a tray of mugs and a plate of biscuits.

'Tsk,' said Bella wagging her finger at Edna, 'What crosses the lips ends up on the hips.' She half-rose to peer over the top of the table at Edna's ample hips, then moved the plate out of her reach.

'I've got the perfect diet regime.' She splayed thumb and little finger as if representing a telephone receiver and mouthed *Phone me*.

'Well, if we can proceed,' said Florrie with a quick glance to her left to check on Bella.

'So, what do we do?' asked Bella.

'The clue's in the name!' snapped the usually peaceful Harriet, picking up her knitting needles. She aimed the points at Bella.

'Indeed,' said Florrie, 'we knit. We natter. We make squares which we sew into blankets for the local dog's home.'

She passed Bella needles and a ball of blue wool. The next blanket *would* be red and blue as Mary had requested. She rubbed the tiny irritated area where until a few minutes ago she'd unknowingly harboured a whisker. Yes, red and blue would definitely do. She'd make sure of that!

'Oh my!' said Bella.

Everyone went rigid, heads moving like meerkats.

'You're knitting a triangle. I thought you said squares?'

Harriet dropped three stitches as she turned, her needles pointing towards Bella and eyed her warily, 'We knit from corner to corner.'

'But I don't know how to do that.'

'Oh dear,' said Florrie, keeping her chin tucked down, 'well, I don't have the pattern on me,' she said pushing her bag containing the patterns further under the table with her foot. 'And we're all decreasing, so no one can demonstrate how to do it. Oh dear.'

Five pairs of needles clickety clacked faster and faster, as if out of control.

'I know,' said Florrie, 'I'll bring the pattern next week. So, rather than waste your precious time now...' She stood ready to escort Bella out, needles still moving so fast, they were a blur.

But Florrie's hint was obviously too subtle for the beautician. She slid her chair closer to Harriet who swung round, needles aimed.

'Umm,' said Rita who was knitting with her hands under the table, 'you could always drop into the dog's home. They've got several of the blankets we've made and there are lots of volunteers there who'd probably love some beauty tips... and your card, of course.'

Five Knitter Natterers collectively held their breath.

'Excellent idea,' said Bella, patting her topknot and then powdering her nose. She smiled benevolently at the ladies. 'Well, no time like the present,' she said and rose to go.

'Mm hmm,' said Harriet, still holding her breath.

Florrie was the first to breathe out. 'Has she gone?'

The high-speed knitting ceased.

'Mm hmm,' said Harriet, gasping.

Florrie took out her lemon-scented air freshener and gave two prolonged blasts in the direction of the door. It was hard to tell if she was attempting to annihilate the beautician's lingering floral scent or whether she was imagining she was firing at Bella herself.

'Thank goodness she's gone,' said Mary.

'I don't know why you're so pleased, Mary, you're the only one who escaped attention.'

Mary's bottom lip trembled. 'Not exactly.'

'Well, she didn't offer you any 'helpful tips', did she?'

'No but I got plenty of attention. I kept feeling her eyes on me. She was looking at me as if I was beyond hope…'

'I think you're being a bit sensitive, dear,' said Rita, her hands curled so her nails were hidden in her palms. 'There's nothing wrong with curly, ginger hair. Honestly.'

'Nor so many freckles,' said Florrie.

'And your face is pleasant being round. It wouldn't suit you to lose much weight,' added Edna eyeing the biscuits.

Mary's bottom lip trembled even more.

'Just as well Gladys wasn't here,' said Rita.

'Oh yes, poor Gladys. Well, at least she was saved the indignity of an encounter with Miss Basilwade. Although...'

'I know,' said Harriet crossing herself, 'I think I'd rather an encounter with Miss Basilwade than go through what poor Gladys has been through. Although I still can't work out exactly what happened.'

'Me neither. I can't understand where the baked beans came into it.'

'No, nor that rabid badger.'

'Badger? I thought it was her lodger.'

'Was her lodger rabid?'

'I don't know. Someone told me it was a wildebeest.'

'Hmm, I'd heard it was a wild beast?'

'Well, one thing's for sure, we won't be seeing Gladys back here for some time.'

'If ever...'

The ladies sat silently with their thoughts for a while.

'Suppose Miss Basilwade comes next week?' asked Edna eventually, 'she might bring wax or... lasers...'

'Suppose she comes to what?' asked Florrie.

'Knit and Natter, of course!'

'No, she won't be able to, because it's cancelled.'

'Since when?'

'Since now.'

'Oh, that's a shame. Surely we're not going to let some botoxed bimbo break up our group?'

'Absolutely not,' said Florrie, 'next week a new group will meet at my house and it will be called… umm… Blankets and Blarney or Squares and Squawk and the membership is firmly closed.'

**About the author**

Dawn's third book *Extraordinary* was published by Chapeltown in October 2017. She has stories published in various anthologies, including horror and speculative fiction, as well as romances in women's magazines. Dawn has written a play to commemorate World War One, which has been performed in England, Germany and France.

www.dawnknox.com

## The Most Visited All Time

The stories in this section are the ones that have been visited most often – ever – and also happen to have been published in 2017.

*It's Never the Same* by Paula R C Readman also comes into this category but of course we've already published that in the Reader's Choice section.

# Mathew 5:38

## Sophie Flynn

### *Flat white*

The woman at the back of the church was beginning to turn heads. Her words created a persistent rhythm; *sorry, sorry, I'm sorry, sorry, sorry*. Subconsciously, people tapped their feet in time to the beat.

The church had been packed when she'd arrived so she'd had to push through. *Sorry*, she'd said, *sorry*, as she wormed her way in, but then the words wouldn't stop; at first, she recited them under her breath, causing only uncomfortable glances from those next to her. But as the vicar began to speak about the boy's once-promising future, tears pooling in his eyes, the words became louder. And louder. They flew out before she could catch them, merging with the sobs of the mourners, *sorry*, fighting against the words of the vicar, *sorry*. Until finally, the vicar stopped; everyone turned.

The chant rang out in declaration: *Sorry. Sorry. I'm sorry. Sorry. Sorry.*

The boy's mother stood up, eyes searching packed pews until, finally, they landed on the chanter. She hadn't expected to see her here. She looked even older. Thinner. Paler. Perhaps that's what happens when you take a life; life must take some of yours in return.

## About the author

Sophie is from the Cotswolds and is currently working on her first novel whilst earning a living as a copywriter and studying for an MA in Creative Writing at Oxford Brookes. She tweets from https://twitter.com/sophielflynn

# Long Black

## Glenn Bresciani

### *A long black coffee*

The cat lover who hates cats, that's what you'd be thinking if you spent a day with my wife and our pet cat.

The cat meowed incessantly. My wife yelled at it to shut-up.

The cat scratched the furniture. My wife's rage could boil pasta.

When a fatal illness left us with no other choice but to have our cat put down, how odd is it that my wife should be the one to lament for two weeks straight. So did she hate the cat when it was alive, yet loved it when it was dead? I can't help but wonder.

Same as with cats, the foster care that we now do also infuriates my wife. So than, does this mean she hates foster children as well? Will she love them when they are gone? Now I'm really confused.

I never did find an answer to this question, but the answer found me when a fifteen year old foster child was placed in our care. Her overuse of eyeliner and black ripped stockings were as Emo as Emo can get. Her name was Lovely and she was delivered to our doorstep by her caseworker, along with all of her belongings stuffed into two swollen trash bags.

This new edition to our family was Lovely by

name, lovely by nature. Yet, no matter how delightful and cordial she was, Lovely had my wife exasperated after one week of being in our care.

'If that girl can't take her clothes out of a trash bag and put them in her wardrobe,' fumed my wife, 'then she can take her trash bags and leave.'

'Why won't you use the wardrobe space in your room?' I casually asked Lovely one night while we watched TV together.

'Why should I,' was her reply. 'I'm only gonna have to move again.'

This poor girl's apprehension became mine as well; sympathy made sure of that. I wanted her in my care forever.

However, a putrid smell oozed out of Lovely's bedroom and the flies began to swarm. Damn! Just as I was starting to get attached, it was over.

A quick snoop through the trash bags and my wife's detective work exposed Lovely's sweat stained, unwashed clothes plus the real reason why the flies had gathered. It wasn't the stink of body odour that attracted the swarm. Oh-no. They came for the packed lunches, forgotten and left to rot in Lovely's school bag. Each bit of food unrecognisable under the layers of fungus and mould.

'Right, that's it,' yelled my wife. 'I'm getting my camera. I want DOCS to see this filth. They can find some other sucker to care for Lovely.'

An urgent phone call to DOCS had Lovely's

caseworker on our doorstep the very next day. She was both apologetic and disappointed. Obviously she has been down this trash bag road before.

'This is the same reason why Lovely was removed from the last three foster homes she was in. If you want her removed from your care then I totally understand.'

What? Get rid of Lovely? Desperate measures called for a creative solution.

'Um… why don't we try a rewards chart,' I suggested. 'You know, give Lovely extra pocket money if she keeps her room clean.'

'That only works on younger children,' criticized my wife, her subtle way of saying: 'I'm done with this.'

The caseworker dissolved all her emotions with a squirt of apathy. It was how she coped with giving Lovely endless bad news. She was about to tell Lovely it was time to go, but then my wife contradicted herself by agreeing to keep Lovely in our care, just to see if my idea would stick.

Sure enough, my idea worked. Turns out even a fifteen year old will keep their room clean to score stickers and extra pocket money.

Lovely's Little Orphan Annie routine only lasted two weeks. The energy and effort required to maintain her blithe persona was too exhausting. So she quit and her true personality was revealed.

Scowls replaced smiles. Abrupt rudeness replaced

chit chat. Just like that, Lovely was lovely to us no more.

Five times I had to ask her to do her chores before she would untangle herself from the social net of Facebook and go wipe the dishes.

She got out of doing her homework by throwing a temper tantrum that would put a toddler's kicking and screaming to shame.

'I'm not paid to do this,' fumed my wife. 'I don't have to put up with this shit.'

The truth is she didn't just put up with Lovely's shit, she also put Lovely's needs before her own. She even worked an extra hour at her crappy retail job to make up for the extra hour lunch break she had to have so she could attend a meeting with the principle of Lovely's high school. The topic the principle wanted to discuss was Lovely's abusive rants at her teachers. He warned my wife that should our foster child persist with her teacher abuse, she will be suspended from school.

Indeed, life was harsh for our angry foster child. Cutting herself with a razor blade was the only way she knew how to cope. When my wife found a blood stained razor blade on Lovely's bedroom floor, she couldn't cope at all.

'Foster care! What the fuck was I thinking?' raged my wife.

Now, I'm guessing by my wife's 'pushed over the edge' reaction, you'd be thinking that Lovely's placement with us was about to be terminated. Well, you'd be wrong. In fact my wife did the opposite by demanding DOCS organise a meeting between us and Lovely's psychologist so we could get a handle on Lovely's detrimental behaviour. For almost two years, Lovely has been seeing this psychologist to help better manage her anger.

'Lovely is a girl with many complex issues,' explained the psychologist, who is hip, metro and loves his metaphors. 'All her issues, every single one, stems from the rejection she has received from all the adults responsible for her well-being.

'Lovely was born to drug addict parents. Now drugs and babies, that's not a good mix. So when a drug overdose had Lovely's father rushed to hospital, DOCS swooped in, snatched Lovely away from her mother and placed her into a foster home. Throughout her childhood, Lovely was told repeatedly by DOCS that– by law – she can never live with her parents until she turns eighteen. And yet, her parents are raising Lovely's younger brother and sister; and yes they still do drugs. The only difference now is that they're not overdosing anymore.

'By the time she hit puberty, Lovely's feelings were like ants swarming out of their nest after it had been kicked in. The dear old lady who was caring for her at the time was frightened of her foster daughter's rage. The poor woman couldn't deal with it so she had Lovely removed from her home.

'Lovely had lived with that carer for thirteen years.

'So you see? Rejection is all Lovely has ever known. This is why she rejects every foster home she is placed in before – in her own mind – she herself is rejected. It has become her self-fulfilling prophecy.'

Wow. It all seemed so hopeless. What could we do? How could we help? The psychologist explained: 'Lovely needs carers who will stay in the boat with her, no matter how many times she rocks that boat and tips it over. It is the only way she will ever build trust again.'

Halfway through the session, the focus of the discussion shifted to my wife – wait! We came here to talk about Lovely. Why are we talking about my wife?

'Hmm. You have all the symptoms of anxiety disorder,' the psychologist said with concern. 'You need to see a psychologist.'

When a psychologist recommends you see a psychologist, you best hurry up and make an appointment to sit on that comfy leather sofa.

The psychologist that my wife chose to visit got straight to the point.

'Are you doing foster care to help pay off your mortgage?'

'No,' my wife replied, shocked by the question.

'Oh. So you do it because you want to. That's interesting. Well, working full time and doing foster care is causing your anxiety. There are two ways a person will react to anxiety; fight or flight. And from what you've been telling me, you're definitely a fighter. Now, if you're serious about reducing your anxiety, I suggest you either quit working full time or quit fostering.'

'No, I have to do both.'

My wife was right. We couldn't do one without the other.

'Okay. Well, I will prescribe to you medication that will take the edge off your anxiety. But more importantly, we need to curb your fighting reflex. To achieve this, I'm going to teach you how to breathe.'

'Breathe?'

'Yes breathing. You do it every second of every day. It costs nothing and if you didn't breathe you would be dead. Buddhist monks have been using breathing techniques for thousands of years. So the next time your anxiety is about to trigger your fight reflex, I want you to stop and breathe. I'll show you how.'

Like Mr Miyagi from Karate Kid, the psychologist trained my wife in the fine art of breathing.

Straight away, my wife's new found mix of Zen and medication was put to the test.

Lovely's caseworker quit DOCS for a new position as a safety inspector for Child Care centres.

The career change had Lovely convinced that she was being abandoned all over again.

A war of retaliation was declared by Lovely on everyone that mattered to her, pushing them out of her life before someone else abandoned her.

Her first target was her psychologist. She quit seeing him on the grounds that their anger management sessions were pissing her off.

Next, Lovely quit high school to distant herself from her most hated enemies. No more pencils, no more books, no more teachers' dirty looks.

For her carers, Lovely used a different tactic. She didn't push us out of her life, she simply cut us off. It was a cruel manoeuvre, I was beyond devastated. We had opened up our hearts to Lovely and she treated us and our home like a boarding house.

So how did my wife fare with all this? I hear you ask. As promised, the medication did its job. Anxiety wasn't her immediate reaction. In fact, she didn't react at all. She just stood still and breathed, again and again until her mind was an expanding emptiness so wide, not even her fight reflex could leap across.

Nevertheless, the final punch in the face to KO Lovely's placement with us came from – of all people – the government.

At sweet sixteen, Lovely was entitled to Youth Allowance, that fortnightly payment of four hundred dollars to be used as financial support for a student's education.

Taking full advantage of the free cash splash, Lovely made the leap from uncooperative to all out renegade. She spent all her allowance on re-inventing herself with Gothic fashion, Vintage fashion; blue hair, pink hair; a new piercing for her already pierced face. From out of the shopping bags she was born again and again.

Gothic paraphernalia and Vintage style dresses piled up on Lovely's bedroom floor. Within a month her room resembled an up ended bin.

On the weekends, Lovely told us that she will be staying the night at her girlfriend's house, but there was no fooling us. We knew when she walked out that front door, she jumped into the car of some nineteen year old boy who was waiting for her at the end of the street. Some weekdays she didn't come home at all. The only times she was ever home with us was when all her Youth Allowance was spent.

Amidst the chaos unleashed by cyclone Lovely, my wife remained centred in mind and spirit, the eye of our foster child's storm.

Suddenly that vast emptiness that expanded to the rhythm of my wife's controlled breathing was no longer empty. My wife wasn't floating in nothing; she was swimming in an ocean of liquid care. All that willingness to care, stretching out to the horizon of my wife's soul, it had been there all along and she never knew. Her anxiety had always ensnared her before she could dive into the oceanic depths of her care.

With her rage now absent and with an abundance of care, my wife did what was right for Lovely – what was right for us all.

It was time for Lovely to go, my wife had decided, but not until she turned seventeen. A teenager at that age has more access to independent living grants. My wife firmly believed that while Lovely was still only sixteen, she should remain in our home so we could bail her out whenever she got herself into trouble.

For almost half a year Lovely stayed with us, until a month after her seventeenth birthday.

DOCS refused to set up Lovely with independent living. Why should they! Just the thought of handing out an independent living grant to a teenager who can't clean up after themselves, let alone keep their room clean – was scandalous. A refuge was all Lovely's new caseworker was going to offer.

Lovely refused the offer, instead choosing to move in with her dad. A new life in a house where the fridge is always empty, she is side stepping the empty syringes scattered across the floor and the couch was all she had to sleep on.

And that was that. Lovely was gone from our lives.

We tried to change Lovely, believe me we did. We encouraged her to do better at school, to think about her future, be more responsible and all those things.

But in the end we failed to make a difference as

Lovely wouldn't listen to anyone, wouldn't trust anyone but herself.

However, the pressure of caring for Lovely exerted change on my wife. Forever free of her anxiety trap, having transcended her fighting reflex, my wife is now unlimited. So too is her capacity to care.

With plenty of care to spare, we now have two teens and one tween living with us in our foster home.

Oh, and one pet cat.

**About the author**

Glenn is an Australian who is a factory worker by day and a writer by night. He and his partner have been caring for foster children for seven years. My stories on foster care have been published on the websites Parenting Express and Next Family.

# Burning Tradition

## Roger Noons

### *A cup of strong tea with just a drop of whisky*

'Edwin wants to see you my Roger.'

'Edwin Davies?'

Rosie nodded and returned to weaving the rope.

'Any idea what for, Rose?'

The Warden of the Travellers Site shook her head, just once. 'Course, old Mrs Davies has passed away.'

'His mother?'

Rosie Watton nodded again. Although she'd held her post for more than five years and I'd visited her on numerous occasions, despite the manner in which she addressed me, I was a Gorgy and hence there was a formality between us; a relationship akin to dentist and patient.

'I'll go and see him.'

It was a fortnight later when I again drove along the lane towards the Site. I was held up following a low loader on which there was the tattiest caravan I'd ever seen. It pulled in through the gateway and passed the Warden's Store. I parked up and went in to see Rosie.

'Who's just brought in that van?'

Again the familiar shake of the grey-haired head as Rosie scurried away to put the kettle on the stove.

'You'll have a cup of tea, my Roger?'

'Thanks Rose, but only tea, thank you. I've to drive back to the office for a meeting.' Rosie's tea was often more Johnnie Walker than Tetley's.

Having concluded my business with Rose, I walked along to where two men had just released the caravan from its ties and were arranging it centrally on the concrete pad which constituted Plot 12. As I watched the low loader was driven away. Edwin Davies appeared from his mobile home on Plot 10.

'All right Boss?'

'Not bad Edwin, yourself?'

'You remember I had a word about…'

'Edwin you said you wanted to carry out the old tradition of burning your mother's caravan following her death.'

'Aye and you said okay as long as we did it after your office closed for the day.'

'This is not your mother's former home.' His face began its beetroot imitation and he shrugged. 'You told me the tradition was to set fire to the van and its contents to prevent the children falling out of who got what.'

Hands in his pockets, Edwin concentrated on kicking loose stones, unprepared to look at me and respond.

Where's your mother's van, Edwin?' I leant towards him so that I heard a muttered 'sold it.'

'You know you have to give up the plot?'

He nodded.

'If there's anything on this site next Monday, I'll charge you a month's rent.'

'Don't worry Boss, it'll be sorted.'

I shook my head as I walked away. So much for Romany traditions.

**About the author**

Roger began writing creatively in 2006, beginning with a screenplay for a film-making friend. Since then he has written more scripts, plays, memoirs and poems. His main output has been short stories, particularly flash and micro fiction. A regular contributor to CaféLit since 2011 with 120 pieces included, his *Slimline Tales* was published earlier this year by Chapeltown Books.

# Workmates

## Roger Noons

### *A mug of builder's tea*

A pale February light crept through the window. At a table in the corner two men played cribbage. The peg board held broken match sticks, like bonsai boles after a hurricane.

The wife of the white-haired man brought mugs of tea and a plate layered with arrowroot biscuits. Neither player acknowledged her nor uttered thanks. Concentration was paramount and although no fragment of weekly pension was being risked, pride overflowed the kitty of counters. The outcome was as important as any cup final.

They had played two afternoons each week since they retired from working at adjacent lathes, wearing identical bib and brace overalls, though different-sized steel toe-capped boots. The venue was always Jack's bungalow as Harry, a widower, lived with his unmarried daughter who treated their dwelling as a prestigious museum. Every surface displayed an exhibit and no speck of dust endured for longer than ten seconds. Harry was embarrassed to invite his friend and Jack was nervous to accept. Maisie, Jack's wife, was happy. Her husband was contented and Harry, for whom she'd always had a soft spot, received a few hours peace.

\*     \*     \*

That late winter afternoon Maisie took a phone call from Harry's daughter.

'Maisie, its Dawn, I'm afraid Dad won't be coming today, he's had a funny turn. I'm waiting for the doctor to come.'

'Oh dear, sorry to hear that, please let us know what the doctor says, and of course if there's anything we can do—'

'I'll ring you as soon as I know something.'

Jack couldn't settle. As soon as Maisie had told him, he was like a moth with a myriad of lights. He went into his greenhouse but could find no chore that needed his attention. In the shed he picked up a saw, but his hand was shaking so couldn't risk damaging it or the wood he was working on. Maisie made him a cup of tea, but it sat on the table adjacent to his armchair.

'I wish she'd ring,' he said to himself, but loud enough for Maisie to hear.

'Sit down, Dawn will let us know as soon as there's some news.'

The five o' clock news bulletin had just begun when the telephone rang. Jack snatched it from its cradle. 'Yes?'

'It's Dawn, the doctor says it was a stroke and he's rung for an ambulance—'

'Right, you go with him and I'll bring the car and

come and find you at the hospital.'

'Thank you Jack.'

The reception desk at The Royal was staffed by volunteers. It was twenty minutes before a sympathetic woman was able to locate the patient. She told Jack that his friend was still undergoing assessment. He sat in the cafeteria with a mug of tea. He watched the comings and goings, feeling he was outside looking in, watching a film the title of which he didn't know.

Almost two hours had passed when Dawn wearily approached him. He stood up, seeing from her expression that she was bearing sad news.

She shook her head and looked away. He held out his arms but she didn't step into them, so he took her elbow and guided her to a chair and watched as hands covering her face, her body shook. He drew up another chair and sat beside her. He offered a handkerchief from the breast pocket of his blazer and eventually as she noticed his action, she took it, whispering her thanks.

Drizzle dulled the scene as mourners gathered at the Crematorium. Within minutes the chapel had filled. Jack avoided using his tuneless voice during the singing of the hymns, in case it deserted him when his turn came to speak.

On hearing his name, he stepped forward opening the pages of his prepared text. When he looked down his glistening eyes found no point of focus. He sniffed, raised his head and set his eyes on the wooden cross over the door by which they had entered.

*Ladies and gentlemen, it's a privilege to talk about Harry Guest, albeit one I hadn't wished for until many years hence. We joined Jennings and Field on the same day fifty two years ago. Young, full of ourselves, eager to learn our trade and compete for places in the Works football team. In fact for ten years we spent weekdays at adjoining benches and Saturday afternoons alongside each other in the familiar red and white strip.*

*He was a quiet man, but when he did speak, it was worth listening. He was generous and modest and what few people know is that he once saved my life. I failed to properly fit a steel rod in the chuck of my lathe and Harry recognising the sound as the job came free pushed me out of the way. He accepted my thanks and a handshake and we never spoke of it again.*

*He was a competitor. Since we retired, we played crib twice every week and although no cash was involved, he loved to win. In fact that, as well as his grin when he pegged out, is what I shall miss most. God bless you Harry and thank you for being a good friend.*

As Jack took his seat, Maisie patted his wrist and offered a handkerchief.

It was six weeks later when Dawn called on Maisie and Jack.

'I found these and wondered if you'd like them?'

124

She handed Jack a black box. When he opened it he found three medals. On the back of one was engraved *John Perry*. Jack frowned, shaking his head.

'Apparently Dad was chosen for the League team and when they presented them at the end of the season, one of them hadn't been inscribed, so he had your name put on.'

'I was never good enough…' Jack could say no more as sobs racked his body.

**About the author**

Roger began writing creatively in 2006, beginning with a screenplay for a film-making friend. Since then he has written more scripts, plays, memoirs and poems. His main output has been short stories, particularly flash and micro fiction. A regular contributor to CaféLit since 2011 with 120 pieces included, his *Slimline Tales* was published earlier this year by Chapeltown Books.

# The Most Visited in the Last 12 Months

These are from the five most visited stories in the last twelve months that also happen to have been published in 2017.

# Crucifix

## Gill James

### *Communion wine*

The sky went black. The cool wind that came along at the same time felt nice. A few drops of rain began to fall. They tickled and made Tom want to giggle.

'I told you we'd have a storm. I said we should have brought our macs,' said Mum. She pulled him and Maisie and Daisy towards her.

'Don't be daft,' said Dad. 'We'd only have had to carry them. This'll be over in no time. It's just a summer storm.'

There was a flash of lightning and then almost immediately a loud bang.

'Is that the clouds bumping into each other?' said Tom. 'That's what Alfie always says.' Alfie was his best friend at school, a bit of a clever clogs. He was usually right about most things, though.

His mum and dad ignored him.

Maisie and Daisy were now clinging on to Mum's skirt. The rain was falling faster now. Their dresses were beginning to stick to their legs and were becoming see-though. Red dye was running out Maisie's dress, making it look as if her legs were bleeding.

'Come on let's get out of this,' said Dad. 'Look, let's shelter in the porch of that church.'

Tom wondered what a church was. He'd seen them before, of course, but he didn't know what they did. He knew all about shops, hospitals and schools but not about churches.

Several other people had had the same idea. It was a bit of a squash in the small doorway. Mum accidentally leant on the big wooden door and it opened a little.

'Oh look,' she said. 'It's not locked. We could go inside. Take the weight off our feet a bit.'

She took the little girls by the hand and ushered them in. Dad guided him from behind.

It smelt funny, a bit like the soil after the rain has fallen on it. The cold seemed to come up through your feet. Maisie and Daisy were shivering now. It was hard to believe that last night none of them had been able to sleep in Mrs Quinn's stuffy old boarding-house.

A few other people sat in some funny chairs that had hard-looing backs.

'You must be really quiet and sit as still as you can,' said Mum. 'These people are trying to pray.'

He didn't understand what that meant. 'What's praying?' he asked.

'Talking to God. They're talking to God,' said Dad.

'What's God?'

Dad sighed. 'Well I don't believe none of it myself. But some people think this very clever man

– God – made everything and it's a good idea to talk to him now and then. That's what churches are for.'

Tom noticed the coloured glass and the paintings on the wall. 'Can I go and look at the pictures?' he said.

'As long as you don't touch anything,' said Dad.

'And don't make a noise,' whispered Mum.

He walked along the narrow passage between the funny chairs and stopped from time to time to look at the pictures, the coloured glass windows or the statues. There were some interesting things here – like the man who was guiding some animals into a great big boat, the tower that was falling down and the bush that seemed to be on fire. 'Dad,' he called. 'Can you tell me what these stories are about?'

'Ssh!' said Dad. 'You mustn't make a noise in Church.

Mum was cuddling the little girls, whispering to them and occasionally stroking their hair. Why didn't she cuddle him like that anymore? Dad stared towards the front of the church and didn't say a word to Mum, or to him or to Maisie and Daisy. The other people sitting in the funny chairs kept their heads bent low.

There was a big table covered with a very posh looking cloth and it had candlesticks on it. There was something near the door that looked like a big stone baby bath. He remembered helping to bath Maisie and Daisy until one day he got soap in Daisy's eyes and she screamed the place down.

'What have you done to her?' Mum shouted.

After that he wasn't allowed to go anywhere near the girls at bath-time.

Never mind. So, you came here if you wanted to speak to God, the really clever man who had made everything. This was incredibly cool. Tom wondered whether he should say something but he couldn't think what and he felt a bit shy actually. Besides, he didn't know exactly where God was.

At the side was a little room without a door and with proper chairs facing away from the main part of the church. Why were the chairs like that? In front of them on the wall was a huge wooden cross and on it a man with nails through his hands and his feet. There was blood coming from them and from his head on which were thorny branches, woven together to look a little like a crown. Oh, it made him feel sick. That must really hurt.

There was a woman sitting on one of the chairs. He couldn't help himself. He just had to know. 'Miss, who's that?'

'That's the Lord Jesus. He's the Son of God. God sent his only son to us. Died for us, he did. So that God would forgive us for being so wicked. He did it because he loves us.'

That was terrible. What a horrible thing to do. Fancy sending your only son away. He was Mum and

Dad's only son. Were they going to send him away? And would somebody put nails though his hands and feet and make him a crown out of brambles?

He screamed. Then he started sobbing. Great breathless sobs.

'There now, there now,' the woman muttered.

Dad came running into the little space. 'What are you making a racket like that for? We told you you'd got to be quiet.' He turned to the woman. 'I'm so sorry.'

The woman shook her head. 'No problem. I was just telling him about what Jesus did.'

'He's cruel, that God. You're not going to send me away are you Dad?'

'He's probably never heard about that before,' said Dad. 'You see, we don't go to church.'

Mum and Maisie and Daisy wandered along.

'I think we can go now anyway,' said Mum. 'I think the rain's stopped.' She pointed to the sunlight that was now streaming through the stained glass windows and making patterns on the floors.

The other people who had been in the church were beginning to shuffle out. They looked away from Tom and his mum and dad and his two sisters. He was probably going to get a ticking off now for embarrassing them.

He took some deep breaths and tried to calm down. He began to hiccough, and each hiccough was followed by a shudder.

It was sunny again outside. The puddles were steaming. The sun was getting warm again but it wasn't so sticky anymore.

'No wonder the kid was scared,' said Dad. 'That figure was as large as life. It looked like something out of a horror film. That's one of the reasons I hate the whole business. And all that stuff about the bread and wine becoming the body and blood of Christ and eating and drinking him. Barbaric!' He ruffled Tom's hair.

Tom really was sure he was going to be sick now. If you went to church you had to eat God's son? No, he must have got that wrong.

'Come on then,' said Dad. 'Let's get going.'

Tom wanted to tell Dad that the man on the cross hadn't frightened him. That he knew it was only a carving and not a very good one at that. It was the idea of God having a son and that son loving everyone so much that he was prepared to let them put nails through his hands and his feet and he would die for him. Would his mum and dad do that for him? Would he do it for them and his sisters?

He couldn't say a word, though. If he did he knew he would start crying again and he didn't want to look like a wimp in front of his dad and his sisters. He'd done enough damage already, getting into a tizzy like that.

'I think the best thing we can do now is go and get an ice-cream, don't you?' said Dad.

The little girls clapped their hands and jumped up and down on the spot. Tom tried his best to smile.

**About the author:**
Gill James writes all sorts of fiction – novels, short fiction, flash fiction and experimental fiction. She is also a publisher and editor.

Visit her blog at www.gilljameswriter.eu

# In MaryWorld

## Dawn Knox

### *Earl Grey tea (because it goes well with fruitcake)*

Mary Wilson dragged a comb through her ginger hair and pulled until the curls surrendered allowing it to reach her shoulders. But when the teeth finally slipped free of the tangles, the hair sprang back to her ears in corkscrew curls. She frowned at her reflection in the mirror. Tight, ginger curls. There was nothing wrong with curly, ginger hair of course. Come the day when she moved to a deserted island and established MaryWorld, curly, ginger hair would be compulsory. It was just unfortunate that at the moment, no one lived in MaryWorld except her. There were lots of facts and truths in MaryWorld that didn't get much credence elsewhere. Or, as Mary's mother put it, 'You're a one off, dear. Completely out of step with the rest of the world. Always been a little madam, haven't you?'

And that wasn't all Mary's mother had to say about her daughter. Take that morning at breakfast, for example.

'If you don't get a move on and find a husband soon—'

'Yes, I know, Mother, I'll be left on the shelf—'

'On the shelf? You'll be lucky to get as far as the shelf. You'll be packed away in some cupboard

134

somewhere with all the rejected—'

'Yes, thank you, Mother.'

'Although…' Mrs. Wilson slid a newspaper cutting across the breakfast table, 'you might rescue things at the eleventh hour. Speed-dating is the new way to meet a man.'

'It's hardly the eleventh hour, Mother! I'm forty-two.'

'Exactly, I rest my case. Forty-two! I was eighteen when I married.'

'Yes but you didn't even like Dad.'

'What's that got to do with the price of fish, eh? At least I wasn't on the shelf at forty-two.'

'Neither am I apparently. I'm in the reject cupboard.'

'Don't be facetious.' Mrs. Wilson tapped the advert… again and again and again.

'Oh all right!' Mary snatched the clipping from the staccato beat of the yellow fingernail.

And that was how she met Derek Carruthers. Not that she'd liked him at first. She might have given in to her mother over the speed-dating evening but she wasn't going to miss the last bus home because of it. Derek had been her last partner and he hadn't made a promising start, remarking that he disliked ginger-haired women. Well, she hadn't liked the look of him either. He had strands of grey hair combed over his bald head like strings on a strangely shaped musical instrument and a florid complexion that she later discovered was caused by his tie being pushed up to conceal the fact that his shirt collar was open because it was too small. Sartorially elegant, he was not. But that was good because Mother would hate his clothes sense and that might be enough to persuade her that Mary should stop seeing him. And then she'd have breathing space until Mother once again remembered Mary wasn't married. But she was getting ahead of herself. They'd only been on one date – if you could call it that. She *had* called it that when telling Mother about it, although it was unlikely that Derek would have seen it as such. While they'd ridden on the last bus back to Basilwade together after the speed-dating event, he'd mentioned that she'd reminded him he needed mouthwash and that the cheapest place to buy some – should she feel the need – and he thoroughly recommended that she did – was Asco's supermarket. Aware that Mother would be critical if she didn't have any positive news from the speed-dating, Mary announced at breakfast that she was going on a date and had then spent most of the following morning prowling the aisles of Asco's in case Derek should appear. She was just about to give up and go home when he rounded the corner, pushing a trolley.

'I'm just buying mouthwash,' she said casually and after that, one thing led to another and they found themselves in the Asco coffee shop.

He'd invited her out for a stroll through

Basilwade on Saturday evening and he'd even bought her a bag of chips. Not that she liked chips but she was quite peckish after their walk and it didn't look like Derek was going to take her to dinner.

She was torn. Derek was definitely not the man of her dreams – there *were* no men in her dreams, indeed none at all in MaryWorld – but in order to keep Mother off her back, she needed to show she was trying.

'… so if you care to come round on Sunday, for tea, you can meet my mother…'

'Whatever for?'

'Well, I live with her, so if you come round for tea, you're bound to bump into her.'

'I see. Well yes, all right then. How long will it take? The Grand Prix is on at half past seven and I never miss it.'

'If you leave at five, I'm sure you'll get home in time.'

Now, how to introduce Derek to her mother? 'Boyfriend' was a ridiculous term. Derek had not been a boy for a long time. If ever. 'Manfriend' sounded just as silly. She'd overheard her next door neighbour's teenage daughter at the bus stop the other day talking about her latest, and she'd used a term… now what was it? She must try to remember. It would be good to sound modern but casual. Slightly committed but not too committed. Yes, she definitely had to establish who Derek was before

Mother started calling him her *intended* or *fiancé*.

Mary had anticipated that Derek would arrive early, so the table was laid and they were already seated when her mother came into the dining room.

'Derek Carruthers,' said Derek standing up and holding out his hand, 'and you must be Mrs. Wilson.'

'How d'you do, Derek…' She fixed him with a steely stare, 'So, you're the man on benefits.'

'I don't believe so,' said Derek sitting down and taking the large slice of fruitcake that Mary offered him.

'Oh Mother! Derek isn't *on* benefits.'

'But you said—'

'I said he was my friend *with* benefits.'

Derek choked, spraying Mrs. Wilson with fruitcake crumbs.

'Well, what on earth does that mean? Benefits? What sort of benefits?' Mrs. Wilson asked, flicking fruit off the front of her blouse.

'Oh, Mother! Honestly, you're so behind the times.'

'That's as may be,' said Mrs. Wilson.

A piece of cake had gone down the wrong way and Derek was finding it hard to breathe. Mary slapped him hard in the middle of his back and with his airway free at last, he clawed at his collar, gasping for air.

'Well, I'm going to take Twinkle for a walk. I think I'll leave you to it,' said Mrs. Wilson picking a half-chewed currant off her sleeve and dropping it on the plate. Whistling for Twinkle, she rose and left.

'*Leave us to it*? You mean…? What, *here*?' asked Derek, '*Now*?'

'Well, yes. Now's as good a time as any.' Mary looked at the enormous cake she'd made that morning. Surely he wasn't going to leave immediately? Mother was enough to intimidate anyone but if he was gone before she got back, it would be obvious the date hadn't gone well. 'Mother will be out for a while. It takes her about twenty minutes to go round the block,' she added, hoping he'd stay at least until she returned.

'Twenty minutes! Look, I'm all for saving time and I know I said I wanted to be gone by five o'clock but this has all been a bit of a shock. I'm sure once I get going it won't take long but I might need a few minutes to summon my… well, to prepare myself… to build myself up, as it were…'

'What for?'

'Well… *it*. You know… *the benefits*.'

Mary didn't know. The only benefit she required was that Derek remained in her life long enough to stop Mother criticising, and then to give her time to realise that her daughter was better off without him.

'More tea? Cake?' she asked weakly.

'Have we got time for tea and cake as well as… it?'

'Well, it's up to you. How much time have you got to spare?'

He checked his watch. 'Hmm. I'm not sure. Only eighteen minutes left until your mother gets back. Suppose she returns before we've finished?'

'Oh don't worry about her,' said Mary looking at the large slab of cake. They definitely wouldn't finish *that* before she got back. 'Look, forget Mother. I know she can be critical but—'

'*Critical?* Critical of what? You're making it sound like she's going to give us marks out of ten!' Derek mopped his forehead.

'Well, she can be a bit demanding but—'

'You haven't got a shot of whisky have you? Or two? I think I need help.'


'Mornin'.' Mrs. Fanshawe from next door rushed to her doorstep when she saw Mary walking down the garden path with Twinkle. 'That was a lot of commotion in your house yesterday afternoon...'

'Yes.' Mary sighed, 'Men are such strange creatures...'

'Oooh, I know. The late Mr. Fanshawe was very peculiar. Who was that man your mum had in a half-nelson? I almost felt sorry for him. Mind you, when she tipped him over the garden gate, he was off like a shot. Never seen anyone so bulky move so fast.'

'Yes, he definitely was a fast mover. Very fast indeed,' said Mary through clenched teeth.

'What! You mean? No! Don't tell me he tried it on?'

Mary nodded.

'With *you?*' Mrs. Fanshawe asked incredulously.

'Yes! With *me!* I was just passing him another slice of fruitcake when he lunged.'

'Oooh I say. The beast! *Lunged*, you say?'

'Yes, *lunged!* His hands were everywhere. Even places I didn't know I had. If mother hadn't come back when she did who knows what might have happened? Mind you in a way it's mother's fault I was in that predicament. She was the one who convinced me to go speed-dating!'

'O-oh!' said Mrs. Fanshawe with sympathy 'Well, why don't you try online dating? That's the way people meet up nowadays.'

'I'm not very confident with computers. I can just about manage to look up the bus timetable but I wouldn't know how to do online dating.'

Mary looked thoughtful. 'Err, You don't think your Amy could help me, do you? She seems to be an Internet expert, she's always got that phone inches from her nose.'

'Well, I could ask her but I don't think she knows anything about dating apps.'

'Yes, I think she does. I was standing behind her at the bus stop the other day and she was telling her friend about someone she'd met online.'

'My Amy? No, I think you're mistaken. She's only sixteen. I'd know if she had a boyfriend.'

'Well, he wasn't exactly a boyfriend. She said he

was her friend with benefits… Mrs. Fanshawe? Are you all right? You seem rather overwrought…'

Mrs. Fanshawe was stomping up the path to the house. 'Ameeee! You get yourself down here right now my girl! You've got some explaining to do!'

Despite Twinkle trying to drag her out for a walk, Mary crept back into the house. Every time she'd mentioned the phrase 'friend with benefits', the world had gone mad. She sat down at the computer and logged on.

Colour drained from her face as she read the definition. So, it was a euphemism for two people who were simply together so they could… Blood rushed back into her face, making her cheeks throb with embarrassment.

Come the day when she moved to a deserted island and established MaryWorld, dating would be banned, men would be banned, mothers would be banned and benefits of any description would be banned. And euphemisms would be banned too.

**About the author**
Dawn's third book 'Extraordinary' was published by Chapeltown in October 2017. She has stories published in various anthologies, including horror and speculative fiction, as well as romances in women's magazines. Dawn has written a play to commemorate World War One, which has been performed in England, Germany and France.

www.dawnknox.com

# Index of Drinks

# Writing For CaféLit

Have you got a story in you? Do you think it would suit CaféLit?

We're looking for thought-provoking and entertaining stories, though ones which might be a tad different from what you normally read in a woman's magazine. They should be the sort of length that would make easy reading whilst you drink a cup of coffee, even if you linger a while, but without you needing to rent a table.

So, perhaps, no more than 3000 words. Shorter stories and flash fiction are naturally very welcome.

We'll read your story. If we like it, we'll let you know and if we don't like it we'll let you know – after a short while. We will work on editing with you.

Each year we'll publish a volume of the best stories. If you are in the volume you will have a share of the profits.

Our editing process will also include some work on your bio to maximise its effect.

We also ask you assign your story the name of a drink. Something light and frothy might be a hot chocolate. A dark piece of flash fiction could be an espresso. Something good for the soul would be a mint tea.

Full submission details can be found at www.cafelit.co.uk/index.php/submission-guidelines-2.

# Also By Chapeltown Books

## "The Best of CaféLit" series

Each story in these little volumes is the right length and quality for enjoying as you sip the assigned drink in your favourite Creative Café. You need never feel alone again in a café. So what's the mood today? Espresso? Earl Grey tea? Hot chocolate with marshmallows?

Order from Amazon:

CaféLit 2011
ISBN: 978-0-9568680-3-9 (paperback) 978-0-9568680-4-6 (ebook)

CaféLit 2012
ISBN: 978-0-9568680-8-4 (paperback) 978-0-9568680-9-1 (ebook)

CaféLit 3
ISBN: 978-1-910542-00-2 (paperback) 978-1-910542-01-9 (ebook)

CaféLit 4
ISBN: 978-1-910542-02-6 (paperback) 978-1-910542-03-3 (ebook)

CaféLit 5
ISBN: 978-1-910542-04-0 (paperback) 978-1-910542-05-7 (ebook)

CaféLit 6
ISBN: 978-1-910542-17-0 (paperback) 978-1-910542-18-7 (ebook)

Chapeltown Books

# Flash Collections

## From Light to Dark and Back Again

## by Allison Symes

This is a collection of flash fiction pieces. The tones vary
from humorous to dark and back again but all reflect
Allison's style of fiction. Some have appeared on CaféLit
(http://cafelit.co.uk) and others on Shortbread Short
Stories. The latter are some of the very first pieces she
wrote years ago, CaféLit is more recent, and other stories
are brand new for this collection.

"This is a quirky collection of flash fiction: from
malevolent fairies to gritty contemporary dramas and bite-
size funny stories. I like the way Allison is playful with
words and gives a fresh slant to traditional tales. A very
enjoyable read."
*(Amazon)*

Order from Amazon:
ISBN: 978-1-910542-06-4 (paperback)
978-1-910542-07-1 (ebook)

# January Stones

## by Gill James

These stories were written one a day throughout January 2013. They were originally published on a blog called Gill's January Stones. Sometimes the stories would come right at the beginning of the day. Sometimes they would take a while longer.

Do they have a theme? Not really, though the idea of 'stones' is one of turning them over slowly on the beach until we find the right one.

There was no strict word count. Each story is as long as it needs to be. It had to be finished, though, by midnight of that day.

"The book is a quirky, easy read and most entertaining. Some of the stories make your blood run cold, others amuse, others are interesting character studies. If you want something a little bit different, this is a great place to start."
*(Amazon)*

Order from Amazon:
ISBN: 978-1-910542-10-1 (paperback)
978-1-910542-11-8 (ebook)

**Chapeltown Books**

# Fog Lane

## by Neil Campbell

*Fog Lane* is a collection of stories about memory. Many of the stories have been published online and in magazines. They were written over a long period of time. The oldest, *The Rose Garden* was first written in about 2007 and published in Orbis. The last one in the book, *Here Comes the Sun*, was completed in 2017. The stories in this book vary from the humorous to the sad to the macabre. They are all short stories of under a thousand words.

Order from Amazon:
ISBN: 978-1-910542-08-8 (paperback)
978-1-910542-09-5 (ebook)

**Chapeltown Books**

# Spectrum

# by Christopher Bowles

A collection of one hundred and ten pieces of flash-fiction and poetry. You probably won't like all of them, and some of them might even disgust you, or make you uncomfortable. But stick with it. Look at overarching themes within each coloured block. Find the puns in certain titles. Research the colours that you've never heard of. Try and work out which stories are complete fabrications, which ones contain nuggets of truth, and which ones are versions of real life events.

Order from Amazon:

ISBN: 978-1-910542-13-2 (paperback)
978-1-910542-14-9 (ebook)

**Chapeltown Books**

# Brightly Coloured Horses

## by Mandy Huggins

Twenty-seven tales of betrayal and loss, of dreams and hopes, of lovers, liars and cheats. Stories with a strong sense of place, transporting us from the seashore to the city, from India's monsoon to the heat of Cuba, and from the supermarket aisle to a Catalonian fiesta. We meet a baby that never existed, a car called Marilyn, a one-eyed cat, and a boy whose kisses taste of dunked biscuits.

"A masterclass in flash fiction" (*Amazon*)

Order from Amazon:
ISBN: 978-1-910542-19-4 (paperback)
978-1-910542-20-0 (ebook)

**Chapeltown Books**

# Potpourri

## by Anusha VR

*Potpourri* is an eccentric mix of stories and poems. Somewhere between working twelve hour shifts at a tax firm and cramming for exams, these stories and poems tumbled onto torn sheets and paper napkins. *Potpourri* is an attempt at preventing the literary world slipping away and regaining a sliver of that bookish world.

Order from Amazon:

ISBN: 978-1-910542-21-7 (paperback)
978-1-910542-22-4 (ebook)

**Chapeltown Books**

# Badlands

## by Alyson Faye

A collection of flash fiction pieces, from drabbles of 100 words to longer pieces up to 1000 words. They reflect an interest in ghost stories, history especially the Victorians, old movies, derelict buildings, real life issues such as homelessness, and just the 'what if' factor of when a seemingly normal situation starts to tilt off centre, dangerously so.

A surprising collection of creepy tales. Tales so twisted, you won't want to read them at night. I didn't, I read them in an afternoon. They are brilliant
*(Amazon)*

Order from Amazon:
ISBN: 978-1-910542-25-5 (paperback)
978-1-910542-26-2 (ebook)

**Chapeltown Books**

# Paisley Shirt

## by Gail Aldwin

*Paisley Shirt* is a fascinating collection of 27 stories that
reveal the extraordinary nature of people and places.
Through a variety of characters and voices, these stories
lay bare the human experience and what it is like to live in
our world.

"I really enjoyed every one of Gail Aldwin's perfectly-
formed little stories, and was hooked from the very
first one."
(*Amazon*)

Order from Amazon:
ISBN: 978-1-910542-29-3 (paperback)
978-1-910542-30-9 (ebook)

**Chapeltown Books**

# Slimline Tales

## by Roger Noons

Each piece has been inspired by something seen, heard
or told about. Much of what you will read is based on
reality and wherever the narrative has strayed from that,
it has been in order to create a story or achieve an
appropriate ending.

If you have time to read this volume from cover to cover,
that's fine. But if you're limited to dipping, moments here
and there to read just a few words, then equally, this slim
volume is for you.

Order from Amazon:

ISBN: 978-1-910542-27-9 (paperback)
978-1-910542-28-6 (ebook)

Chapeltown Books

# Our first children's picture book

## of which we're immensely proud

### Who Will Be My Friend?

### by Colin Wyatt

*Who Will Be My Friend?* is a story about friendship, aimed at children approximately three to eight years of age. It features a Baby Bunny who is lonely and is looking for a friend to play with. Although the bunny meets lots of other animals, because of their differences they give him reasons why they can't become his friend. Finally however, Baby Bunny does succeed and finds a friend to play with and is never lonely again.

Order from Amazon:

ISBN: 978-1-910542-12-5 (paperback)

**Chapeltown Books**

Lightning Source UK Ltd.
Milton Keynes UK
UKHW020735140319
339130UK00009B/472/P